The Best Christmas

The Best Christmas

Jane B. Mason and Sarah Hines Stephens

SCHOLASTIC INC.

New York Toronto London Auckland Sydney
Mexico City New Delhi Hong Kong Buenos Aires

ISBN 0-439-68371-8

Copyright © 2002 by Jane B. Mason and Sarah Hines Stephens. All rights reserved. Published by Scholastic Inc. SCHOLASTIC, APPLE PAPERBACKS, and associated logos are trademarks and/or registered trademarks of Scholastic Inc.

12 11 10 9 8 7 6 5 4 3 2   5 6 7 8 9/0

Printed in the U.S.A.   40

First Scholastic paperback printing, November 2004

*For Leila Hoefling, Beverlee J. Thivierge,
Norma Lind, Madge Frostman, Lillian Morey,
and Pauline Rothenbueler.
Many thanks for sharing your time and your stories.*

Contents

The Best Christmas

Chapter One
December

Hattie pushed open the door to the barn with a mighty shove. Inside, it was cold. The walls kept out the icy gusts, but not much more in the winter.

Rusty strutted up to her as she closed the door behind her. Rusty was the most temperamental banty rooster Hattie had ever known. If you didn't greet him first thing, he'd sulk all day long.

"Hello, Rusty," she said, letting him peck at her boot. "Are you trying to wish me a Merry Christmas?"

Christmas. Hattie felt funny even saying the word out loud. Of course, there were still weeks left until the big day came. But usually Hattie started feeling excited about the holiday right after Thanksgiving. Usually she was the one clamoring to get out the decorations and light the candles in the windows as soon as Thanksgiving was past. And here it was, well into December. So why didn't it feel like Christmas?

Making her way across the big barn, Hattie patted the horses and broke the ice that had formed overnight on their water. She gave the pigs the little bit of slop she'd brought from the kitchen, then headed back to check on the cows and get the feed.

The three cows were lean and dry — it had been weeks since they'd given enough milk for her or her little brother, Dodge, to get even a glass of it. Hattie missed the milk, but was relieved not to have to help with the milking.

Hattie climbed the ladder to the hayloft and tossed down a few forkfuls of hay. She wished she could toss down some extra to give the cows a treat, but she knew there was no such thing as "extra" anything. Not even a forkful of hay. Not on her aunts' farm. Not this year.

Hattie scrambled down from the loft and started to measure out feed for Chestnut and Honeycomb, the horses. There was a lot to do in the barn in the mornings. Hattie knew she shouldn't complain. On the farm everyone worked hard. And they were doing a lot better than most families. But she couldn't help it. *If Papa were here*, Hattie thought, *maybe things would be different.*

Hattie's father had been traveling the country on and off for nearly two years — ever since they'd come to live on the aunts' farm. Papa said he wasn't a farmer, that he could do the family more good looking for work in other places. So he traveled, trying to sell pots and pans and ribbons and anything else he could to make some cash to pay the farm's loans. Cash was hard to come by, and not just in Wisconsin. The whole country had fallen on hard times.

It always comes back to money, Hattie thought. If only she could make some money, then maybe Papa wouldn't have to be gone so far and so often.

Papa hadn't made it home for Thanksgiving. And Christmas was coming whether it felt like it or not. Hattie hoped he'd be back for Christmas. But deep down she was afraid he wouldn't. His last letter had come from California — an awfully long way from Wisconsin.

If he makes it home, Hattie resolved, *I'll make sure he stays a good long while.* But that would take money, Hattie knew.

Hattie had been working on a plan all summer to keep Papa home. She'd picked and sold quart after quart of blueberries. She had made quite a bit of money. But there weren't any berries in the winter. If she could just think of a way —

"How you doin' there, Shortcake?"

Hattie was so lost in her thoughts that she jumped when she heard the familiar voice. It was Abe, one of the men who lived in the converted bunkhouse out back. He and Frank helped Aunt Ruth work the farm in exchange for food and a place to live. He always called Hattie "Shortcake," even though she was taller and skinnier than most kids her age.

3

"You counting those oats by hand?" Abe pushed Hattie's hat down so it covered her eyes.

"I was just . . ." Hattie started to explain, but Abe nudged her away from the grain sacks with his shoulder and gently took the scoop from her hand.

"You were just getting off to school, I think. Go on. I'll finish up here."

"Thanks, Abe." Hattie smiled and straightened her hat. When she opened the barn door she nearly tripped on Rusty, who let out a squawk.

"Sorry, Rusty!" Hattie said, closing him back inside the barn. The sun was high, glinting on the ice. She must have been daydreaming for a while, which meant she was late. And cold. And feeling a bit like a temperamental banty herself.

Aunt Polly was waiting for Hattie in the kitchen. Her dark blond hair was tied neatly into a bun at the nape of her neck. She smiled warmly at her niece.

No matter how cold or early it was or how bad things looked, Aunt Polly was always cheery. Hattie wished she could be cheery all the time like that. But she just wasn't. Everyone said she was more like her Aunt Ruth: practical and grumbly.

A bowl of cold oatmeal was waiting on the kitchen table. Dodge had already left for school — a two-mile walk. Since he was only six, he didn't do barn chores in the morning. He did chores around the house, like bringing in wood for Aunt Polly.

4

Hattie didn't even take off her coat to gulp down her breakfast. She didn't want to be late.

"Don't choke, now," Polly cautioned as her niece shoveled in the cereal.

"Aren't you gone yet?" Aunt Ruth scolded, coming in with a blast of cold air. Aunt Ruth looked nothing like her sister Polly — except for the blue eyes. She had short hair, dark like Hattie's, and her skin was deeply tanned from working in the field.

"I'm trying to be," Hattie said through her last mouthful of oatmeal.

"Well, don't think I'm going to offer you a ride. I've got to get over to check on the new neighbors this morning."

Hattie hadn't expected a ride. And she wasn't late on purpose!

Grabbing her books and lunch (and managing a smile for Polly), Hattie was out the door.

She ran until a stitch in her side made her slow down. She *really* didn't want to be late. Today Miss Lind would be assigning parts for the Christmas show and Hattie wanted to stay on her good side. Hattie was hoping to do "The Night Before Christmas." Her mama had recited it for her every Christmas Eve before she died. It was Hattie's absolute favorite Christmas poem, and she already had it nearly memorized. Miss Lind was bound to pick her.

Hattie could see the smoke curling from the chimney of the one-room school. She could also hear the bell

5

ringing. She was late. Her feet were freezing and her lungs ached, but she ran the rest of the way anyway.

Warming her nose with her mitten, Hattie pushed open the door as quietly as she could. She went to take her place in the second row. Only she couldn't — there was someone else sitting at her desk. A new girl!

"Hattie, I wasn't sure you were coming," Miss Lind said. "This is Lily Swenson. She's our new student — and your new neighbor, I think."

The new girl smiled broadly at Hattie. She was wearing a pretty yellow gingham dress and her blond braids were tied off with matching yellow ribbons.

Hattie was too irritated to smile back. She looked at the floor and mumbled hello before placing her lunch pail by the stove next to the others. How could Miss Lind give her seat away?

"Why don't you take the empty seat next to Henry today?" Miss Lind continued. "We'll get the seating sorted out later."

Hattie moved reluctantly away from the fire toward the empty seat on the other side of the room.

"Hurry now, you've already made us late in getting started," Miss Lind coaxed.

Hattie hurried, and quickly slumped down in the empty seat before anyone could see her scowl.

Chapter Two

The New Girl

Nothing about the day was going as Hattie had planned. Miss Lind passed back the penmanship papers, and Hattie got a C along with a little note that said, "Harriet, you can do better."

Usually Hattie did very well in school. More than once Miss Lind had read her papers out loud to the class. But penmanship? Hattie just didn't see the point of all those loops and curlicues. Still, she hated to disappoint her aunts and her teacher.

During history Hattie tried to show Miss Lind that she could do better by raising her hand whenever she knew the answer. Maybe Miss Lind couldn't see Hattie as well in the back of the room. But she called on Lily twice. Hattie decided to leave her hand up all the time, to increase her chances of getting called on. She usually knew the answer.

After a few minutes Hattie's arm was tired. She propped her left elbow on the desk and used her hand to hold up her right elbow. That was better. And it kept her hand from waving around so much.

"Yes, Hattie?" Miss Lind asked. "Did you have a question?"

Hattie put her arm down quickly. In her effort to keep her hand up, she'd obviously missed something. Miss Lind wasn't looking for answers anymore and Hattie had to think of a question — fast. She felt her face going red as everyone turned to look at her.

"May I go to the bathroom?" she asked. She couldn't think of anything else.

"Of course," Miss Lind said, giving Hattie a funny look.

Hattie jumped up, grabbed her coat, and ran out of the room feeling more humiliated than ever. Of all the stupid questions she could think of! By the time Hattie had walked to the outhouse and back it was recess and all the kids were eating lunch at their desks.

To get her lunch from behind the stove Hattie had to squeeze by the crowd that had gathered around her old desk, which Lily had taken.

"Tell us about Duluth," she heard someone ask. But before Lily could answer everyone had something to say.

"My uncle took me to Duluth once," Karin Withers spoke up.

"Is it true they've got more than half a dozen talkie movie theaters?" Jenny Soma asked.

"Do they drive cars all winter?" Billy Sanders chimed in.

"Lots of people drive in the winter, but you can take streetcars, too," Lily answered. "You can get from one end of the city to the other on the streetcars."

She sure loves the spotlight, Hattie thought. *But doesn't she get tired of answering questions?* It's not like Lily Swenson was the only person who'd ever seen a city. Hattie had been to Duluth, too — even if it was when she was five. And it was a lot easier to get there now since they'd finished paving Highway 2.

When the students were done eating, everyone bundled up and tromped outside for some fresh air. Lily still had a crowd around her.

Hattie grabbed the big sled that was leaning against the wall by the stairs outside. "Anybody want to take a few runs?" she yelled. Usually there was a whole pack of sledders ready to zoom down the hill behind the school — everyone but the little kids. This time, Hattie didn't get a single response.

"I'll go," Dodge offered quietly. Hattie hadn't realized her little brother was standing beside her. She looked at his green eyes for a second, then stomped back into the empty schoolhouse.

"Forget it," she mumbled. Why would she want to sled with her kid brother? He hadn't even saved her seat this morning!

Furious, Hattie tugged off one woolen mitten. Her day could not get any worse. With a huge sigh, she pulled a folded piece of paper from her coat pocket. It was the most recent letter from Papa. She opened it carefully — it was almost coming apart at the creases from being folded and refolded so many times. She started to read.

November 20, 1934
San Francisco, California

Dear Hattie and Dodge,
  By the time you get this letter it will be Thanksgiving. I wish more than anything that I could be there with you to taste some of Polly's good cooking and squeeze you both in a mighty bear hug, but I'm not going to be able to make it.
  Please don't be cross with me. (Harriet, I can almost see your eyebrows coming together on your forehead just the way your mama's used to!) I had planned to come home for Thanksgiving, but I got wind of opportunity in California, so that's where I am now. It was an ill wind, I'm sorry to say. The stories I heard of work and money were nothing but fairy tales.
  The Golden State is beautiful and the Great Central Valley is surrounded by hills so smooth they look like knees under a green blanket. (There's grass growing in November!) But California is as bad off as all of the other states I've been through. Maybe worse.

There are families blowing in every day who caught scent of that same wind I did — families whose farms in Oklahoma dried up — people who packed everything they had and rode out to find that there are no jobs. Now they are out of money and have no place to go.

When I talk to these families about where they've been and what they've seen, I feel I am a lucky man. At least I have a home to go back to.

It may seem like there's not much to be thankful for this year, but deep down I'm sure you know there is. We have our health, and no matter how far apart we are, we have one another. More than anything we should be thankful that we have your mama's sisters and their fine farm.

I had hoped to have some money to send your aunts to keep the Lofstroms off their backs, but I didn't find it here in California. I'll be heading east soon. I've heard good things about the Great Salt Lake in Utah. Perhaps there will be something for me there.

I think of you every day.

> *Love,*
> *Papa*

Hattie refolded the letter and tucked it back into her coat pocket. She looked at the big map of the United States hanging behind Miss Lind's desk. Her chest felt tight, like it might split right open if she took a deep breath.

California was much too far away.

Even if Papa was headed in the right direction, there was no way he'd make it home for Christmas. And he hadn't said anything about it in his letter.

When the other kids rushed back in and noisily took off their coats, Hattie hardly heard them. She hung up her own coat and took her new seat in a daze. It wasn't until Miss Lind started picking students for the Christmas program that Hattie perked up a little.

Hattie's mama always said that when you wished really hard for something, you should hold your thumb in your fist for luck — but never hold two thumbs, only the left one, closest to your heart.

Hattie held her left thumb so tightly it hurt and silently recited what she knew of "The Night Before Christmas." She had to get picked for that poem. She just had to.

"Who knows 'The Night Before Christmas'?" Miss Lind turned to face the class. Hattie's hand was up first, but Jenny Soma raised her hand quickly, too. And right behind them was Lily.

Hattie bit her lip and squeezed her thumb until she thought it would fall off. She even crossed the fingers on her right hand for double luck.

"Lily, why don't you try it," Miss Lind finally said. She wrote Lily's name on the board.

Hattie could not believe her ears. In just one day the new girl had stolen her seat, her school friends, her favorite teacher, and her Christmas recitation.

As the rest of the kids were given parts, Hattie could only watch and listen. She did not raise her hand again. Dodge was given a solo on his nickel horn in the Teeny Weeny Band. Jenny was going to play Mary in the Nativity. Everyone had something good to do.

"I guess that's it," Miss Lind said, wiping her hands on her skirt and looking at the list on the board. "Oh, wait. Hattie, you don't have a part yet, do you?"

Hattie shook her head. She wasn't holding out much hope, but *something* had to go right today.

"We'll have to fix that." Miss Lind picked up her chalk. "I know," she said after a moment. "You can be the Archangel."

Hattie tried to smile, but the truth was, the Archangel was a terrible part. She remembered last year when David got it. He only had one line, and a torn bedsheet for a costume.

Henry, next to her, poked her on the elbow. "You got off easy," he said. "You barely have to say anything!"

With a groan, Hattie put her head down on her desk.

Chapter Three
Hattie's Plan

"Wait up!" Dodge called. Hattie was already a good way down the road toward home when her brother emerged from the schoolhouse. She did not want her awful day at school to last even one minute longer.

"Well, hurry." Hattie slowed her pace, but didn't stop. She was impatient to get home.

During the last lesson all she could think about were blueberries.

"Wait . . . wait!" Dodge was slightly out of breath and his shoe was untied.

"We all ride streetcars in Duluth," Dodge continued, jogging up behind her and twirling a pretend braid. "But everybody has a car, too, and we drive them to the talkies every night."

Hattie laughed in spite of herself. Dodge's imitation of Lily was almost perfect.

When they got home, there were chores to do — snow to shovel and firewood to bring in. Afterward,

Hattie helped Aunt Polly with supper while Dodge set the table.

Pulling up the big wooden floor panel, Hattie tromped down the steep steps to the root cellar to get some vegetables for Aunt Polly. Down under the house it was dark and cool, but not as cold as outside. Crates on both sides of the steps held apples, carrots, potatoes, and rutabagas. Pickles and kraut barrels stood against the back wall. And off to the side were rows of canned tomatoes, corn, peas, beets, and applesauce — the fruits and vegetables Ruth and Polly grew in the summer. But Hattie barely noticed them. Instead she went right over to the blueberries.

It had been a great summer for blueberries — almost too many to pick. The bushes had been so full that the squabbles about blueberry territory between the local Indian tribes and the white people had been few and far between.

All through August Hattie had picked and picked and picked. She had picked until her back ached and her fingers were stained blue, even after she washed them three times. Hattie had sold most of her berries. All but the ones on the shelf.

Quickly and quietly, Hattie split the jars of berries into two burlap sacks and stashed them by the barrels. The blueberries were hers. She was the one who had picked them, and she was the one who had canned them, too (with a little help from Aunt Polly). Still, she felt funny taking food from the family larder.

She remembered the last time Polly made muffins. Ruth had asked, "Are these Hattie's berries?" and Polly had said yes. Hattie was proud to share them then. Now it was time to do something else with them. Hattie was sure that once the aunts saw that she was sacrificing the berries to keep her papa home, they would understand. Until then, Hattie decided she would keep her plan a secret.

At dinner, Aunt Ruth told them all what she'd seen over at the Swensons' farm.

"They don't know what they're doing, but I reckon they'll be okay if they can get through the winter," Ruth reported. "And they said they have food laid up. Lord knows they'll need it."

"Things must have been pretty bad for them in the city," Polly said, shaking her head. "I know it would take a lot to make me leave my home."

Hattie remembered two years back when she and Dodge and Papa had moved from Iron Creek out to the farm to live with the aunts — not too far. Things were bad then. That was after Mama died.

Hattie missed her home, but the feeling paled in comparison to how much she missed Mama. Papa often reminded her and Dodge how lucky they were that Mama had three sisters who loved them and wanted to look after them. And they *were* lucky. Mama's older sisters, Aunt Polly and Aunt Ruth, and her younger sister, Aunt Stella, were all just a little bit like Mama. Though nobody could ever take Mama's place, her sisters were the next best thing. Still, Hattie knew all too well it took something awful to make a family leave their home.

On Saturday Hattie woke up before Rusty had made it to the barn loft for his morning crow. Today she would put her plan into action.

Bracing herself, she threw back the covers and leaped out of bed. The wood floor felt like ice under her bare feet. Hattie dashed across the room, grabbed her clothes from the chair, and dove back under her quilt and blankets. She changed her clothes underneath the covers before stuffing her nightgown inside her pillowcase and hurriedly making her bed.

Dressed, Hattie pulled a partially full mason jar from under her bed and dumped it out on her quilt. Her summer blueberry money. She counted each dime, nickel, and penny — four dollars and three cents. Enough money to keep Papa home for at least a few days. If everything went right, maybe she could get him to stay for a whole week.

Hattie quickly put the money back into the jar and stuck it under her bed. She had to get moving if she was going to make it to town. It was a long walk, and there was no chance of getting a ride. Frank and Abe would probably need the buckboard for chores around the farm. And even if she could talk Ruth into using the gasoline, the family car was already up on blocks for the winter.

Hattie was done with her chores long before breakfast. Aunt Polly didn't see her slip in and out of the root cellar. So far everything was going well. Hattie almost couldn't help grinning as she quickly set the table.

"What's your rush, Shortcake?" Abe came in the kitchen door followed by Frank. They joined the family for most meals. Out in the bunkhouse they only had a regular woodstove — not a cookstove. Hattie wasn't sure they knew how to cook much anyway.

A long time ago, Abe had been married and owned his own farm, but after his wife died he didn't have the heart to keep up his farm alone. When the bank took Abe's farm away, Aunt Ruth asked him if he would come work for her. Abe said Ruth was his guardian angel and went on and on about her generous act of charity, taking in an old man.

"Some angel," Ruth always snorted in reply. "This isn't charity, this is a job. I hired you to work." And work he did. In the summer Polly used to send Hattie and Dodge out to the fields to drag Abe and Ruth in for supper. Often that wasn't even enough and Polly would go after Ruth and Abe herself, chasing and swatting them with her dish towels toward the kitchen like wayward cows.

Frank's story was a little different. He'd come knocking on the door the way lots of single men did — looking for work, maybe just enough to earn a home-cooked supper. Polly fed lots of wandering men out the back door of the kitchen that way, but Frank didn't just come and go.

Hattie remembered the day he'd arrived. She'd been in the barn with Dodge when she heard Aunt Polly's tinkly laugh. Dodge and Hattie both scrambled to see what was so funny — usually Dodge was the one who got the giggles started at the Best farm.

There was Aunt Polly, red-faced and laughing, leaning on the doorjamb to hold herself up while a tall, skinny man with curly dark hair smiled down at his worn boots beside her. A little while later Frank was chopping kindling. Even after he'd had his meal, Hattie noticed he was in no hurry to leave.

After she'd gone to bed, Hattie heard her aunts talking late into the night and opened her door to listen.

"You need the help," Polly said.

"We're doing fine," Ruth snapped back.

"There's room in the bunkhouse and all he wants are his meals and a roof."

"We don't have enough food —" Ruth started to protest.

"We do so!" Polly raised her voice. "What do you know about the larder? I'm the one who's always in it. We have more than enough food and more than enough work! You can't run this whole farm with the help of one old man, a widowed sister, and two children, Ruth."

For a moment nobody spoke. Then Polly cleared her throat.

"And besides, I already told Frank he was hired."

Nothing more was said.

Polly rarely fought with Ruth and almost never raised her voice. But when she did, it seemed like Polly was the older sister.

Hattie was glad Polly had hired Frank. The only problem was that he liked to tease even more than Abe!

"Where's the fire?" Frank asked when Hattie sloshed the milk pitcher onto the table before sitting down.

Hattie didn't want to tell anyone about her plan. She didn't want to give anyone the chance to talk her out of it.

"I was just hoping to get into town today. I want to find Miss Lind and ask her about my part in the Christmas show so I can practice." Miss Lind helped out in the general store on Saturdays.

"But you've only got one —" Dodge started to say. Hattie kicked him under the table, cutting him off.

"I was hoping you kids could help me in the hayloft today," Aunt Ruth said, leaning back in her chair. She folded her strong arms across her chest and focused her blue eyes on Hattie.

Hattie felt her heart sink down around her knees. She looked at her corn bread and what was left of her fried apples. She had to get to town *today*.

Polly shot Ruth a look across the table.

"But if you take Dodge and get home in time to do your chores before supper, I guess I can manage," Ruth finished.

"Great!" Hattie jumped up, knocking the table. She immediately sat back down. "May I be excused?" she asked. "And, um, thank you."

Frank and Abe couldn't hide their chuckles behind their coffee mugs. Hattie didn't care. She didn't even care that she had to take Dodge with her.

"Finish your corn bread and then you can be excused," Polly said with a smile.

"What's in the bags?" Dodge asked, pointing at the two lumpy burlap sacks Hattie had slung over her shoulders.

"Nothing," Hattie replied as she tightened her scarf around her neck. It was windy outside.

"They look awful heavy for nothing. Do you want me to carry one?" Dodge offered.

Hattie wasn't too sure about Dodge's secret-keeping skills. "Nah, you'll just drop it," she told her brother.

"Will not."

"Will too." Hattie could see her breath. But not even the cold or the bickering or the long walk ahead could spoil her good mood.

"Hattie, look! Here comes Abe!" Dodge yelled.

Abe rode up behind them with the buckboard and horse team.

"Can I offer you travelers a lift to town?" Abe winked.

"Can I hold the reins?" Dodge asked as he scrambled onto the seat beside Abe.

"We'll see," Abe said, smiling and looking back to make sure Hattie got in all right. Hattie and Dodge both knew that meant yes.

"Thanks, Abe," Hattie said as she gently lowered her sacks into the back and climbed up the wheel and over the side after them. Abe coaxed the horses back into motion and handed Dodge the reins.

This is perfect, Hattie thought.

Now she would have plenty of time to put her plan into action.

Chapter Four

A Trip to Town

Abe dropped the kids off in front of the Iron Creek Co-op Mercantile. Full of hope, Hattie jumped down and gently lifted the burlap sacks off the springy boards.

"I've got some business to attend to," Abe said. "You kids be careful, and I'll see you back at the farm this afternoon."

Hattie nodded and watched as Abe's silver hair disappeared down Main Street. Maybe he was working on some Christmas surprises of his own.

Dodge was about to open the co-op door when Hattie stopped him.

"You have to wait here," she told him. "I've got some business, too."

Dodge scowled. "It's freezing out here!" he complained, wrinkling up his nose.

Hattie felt bad, but only for a second. She couldn't have Dodge interfering with her plan. Somehow he'd mess it up. Dodge was always messing things up. "You're out of the wind," she told him. "And it will only be a few minutes."

Hattie didn't wait for her brother to answer. She opened the door to the mercantile and stepped inside.

The Co-op Mercantile was one of Hattie's favorite stores. They sold practically everything, and the walls were lined with shelves of fabrics, canned foods, and household goods. Of course, nowadays, the shelves weren't as full as they used to be. The stuff on them didn't seem to change much. People mostly bought the things they really needed: flour, sugar, spices, and maybe a little coffee.

As she made her way to the front counter, Hattie didn't see anyone in the store — except for the big orange tabby cat asleep on top of the cracker barrel. Opening her bags, she carefully pulled out six jars of canned blueberries. She lined them up neatly on the long wooden counter.

During the summer Matilda Laukkanen bought quarts of Hattie's berries for twelve cents apiece. Matilda ran the mercantile with her husband, Hugo. Together they shipped the blueberries to Duluth, and even Minneapolis and Chicago.

Hattie gazed at the six quarts and thought about all of the pies and muffins they could make during the winter. Nothing tasted better than a warm slice of blueberry pie in January. But that was nothing compared to having — and keeping — Papa home. It was worth it to sell the blueberries to Matilda instead.

Just as Hattie finished putting the jars in a row, Matilda came out from the back.

"Why, Hattie Best!" Mrs. Laukkanen exclaimed when she saw Hattie. "What a treat it is to see you!" She bustled forward, flipped up a section of the long wooden counter, and gave Hattie a hug. It was a big hug, because Mrs. Laukkanen was a big woman. She talked a lot, too. Customers liked her.

"How are Polly and Ruth? Busy getting ready for Christmas, I suppose. And what about Stella?"

Stella was Hattie's aunt who had moved away. She and Mrs. Laukkanen had grown up together and were in the same grade in school.

"We haven't heard from Aunt Stella in three months," Hattie admitted. "But Aunt Ruth is betting she'll be stopping by before too much longer."

"Well, when she does, you tell her hello from me. I haven't seen Stella Ecklund in far too long." Matilda smiled down at Hattie. "And what about your papa?"

Hattie explained that she and Dodge got letters from Papa almost every month, and that his last letter came from California. "It's awfully far away, but I'm hoping he'll make it home for Christmas."

Mrs. Laukkanen gave Hattie's shoulder a gentle squeeze. "I'm sure he'll get home if he possibly can," she said warmly. "Now, what brings you to town?"

"Well, I was hoping to earn a little extra money," Hattie started to answer. She stopped when she saw Mrs. Laukkanen's face. As soon as the friendly woman spotted the jars of blueberries on the counter, her wide smile suddenly looked a little sad.

"They certainly are beautiful berries," Mrs. Laukkanen said, picking up a jar and looking it over. "I don't see a single stem. But I'm afraid I'm all stocked, and with the snow already here I can't ship them to the cities like I can in the summer and fall." Mrs. Laukkanen let out a sigh. "I'm sorry, Hattie."

Hattie felt a lump in her throat, but she managed a weak smile. In five seconds, her entire plan had been smashed. Papa would never be able to stay home now.

"Oh, that's okay," she assured Mrs. Laukkanen. "I just thought I would ask."

Hattie repacked the jars into her sacks and started back down the main aisle.

"Say hello to your aunts for me," Mrs. Laukkanen called as Hattie pushed open the heavy door.

"I will," Hattie called back, trying to sound cheerful.

The cold air hit Hattie in the face as she stepped onto the mercantile porch. She felt saggy, like a three-day-old balloon. Then she saw the front porch was empty.

Where was Dodge?

"Edward Hamilton Best," Hattie growled, sounding an awful lot like her Aunt Ruth, "what have you gotten up to?" Her little brother was constantly stirring up trouble, and right now she'd had enough.

She looked up, down, and across the street. Dodge was nowhere to be found.

Starting to panic, Hattie stepped off the porch onto the sidewalk. That's when she heard the mercantile door close behind her. Had Dodge gone in after her, even though she'd told him to wait outside?

Hattie whirled around, ready to let Dodge have it. But it wasn't Dodge. It was Lily Swenson!

"Is everything okay?" the new girl asked, coming toward Hattie. Her hat was stylish and trimmed with fur. Her round blue eyes were full of concern.

Hattie was so horrified she didn't know what to say. Lily had been in the co-op the whole time, and had heard absolutely everything!

Chapter Five
Carlbom's Candy Kitchen

Hattie was so surprised — and so annoyed — that she didn't say anything. Lily, though, started babbling right away.

"I know what it feels like to need extra money for Christmas presents," she said. "When I lived in Duluth I was always trying to get more allowance in December."

Allowance? Hattie didn't know anybody who got an allowance. Kids just did what they could to help out.

"You know," Lily went on, "just a little more than my regular allowance, which isn't much, if you ask me." Lily rolled her eyes.

Hattie didn't know what to say. She didn't *want* to say anything. She just wanted Lily to disappear — poof! — into thin air.

"I have to look for my brother," Hattie blurted. She decided the best place to search was Carlbom's Candy Kitchen, and started off in that direction.

Lily followed her, still talking away. "In Duluth we'd make wreaths and Christmas decorations for change, and sometimes sell little Christmas cakes. We'd spend all morning making stuff, and all afternoon selling it door-to-door. Pumpkin spice cake is my favorite. What's yours?"

Hattie didn't answer. She just kept walking. Three more doors and she'd be there. A gust of wind made her pull her hat down over her ears. It was cold today.

"Anyway, one year I made almost a dollar. I was so excited! I bought the best Christmas presents and lots of candy."

Hattie couldn't believe it. Didn't this girl know when she wasn't wanted? She looked over and saw that Lily was moving her head this way and that while she talked. Her nose was all red, making her eyes look even bluer. The cold didn't seem to bother her.

"That candy lasted until the end of January — four whole weeks!"

Hattie was getting mad. Really mad. She didn't want pocket money or penny candy. She wasn't worried about buying Christmas presents. She was trying to save her family!

"I was very impressed with myself, actually," Lily went on.

Just outside the Candy Kitchen, Hattie whirled around. "This isn't Duluth," she half-shouted, a little louder than she meant to. "And people around here don't buy wreaths, Christmas decorations, or cakes. They make their own!"

Lily stepped back, her mouth hanging open.

Color rising in her cheeks, Hattie whirled back around and yanked open the door to Carlbom's, pulling it quickly closed behind her. She was just in time to see Dodge stuffing a handful of licorice bites into his mouth.

Dodge looked up, his lips stained black from the candy. His curly blond hair was all staticky from the dry winter air. "Hi, Hattie," he mumbled sheepishly.

Hattie stormed up the aisle. "Dodge!" she whispered fiercely, glaring at him with her big hazel eyes. "How are you going to pay for this?" She pointed to the two bites left in his hand and the black goo around his mouth.

"Why, hello, Hattie," Mr. Carlbom greeted her. "Don't you worry, I told Dodge he could have some. There's no charge."

Hattie was about to heave a huge sigh of relief. The way things had been going, she needed something good to happen. But then she remembered Papa's and Aunt Ruth's strict rule about charity. They couldn't accept *any* charity from *anybody*.

Unfortunately, Hattie didn't have any money with her. She'd been planning to *make* money today, not spend it. And, of course, Dodge didn't have any, either. He always spent his money the second he got it.

With a pang, Hattie remembered her blueberries.

She opened one of the sacks and set a jar on the counter. "We can't accept free candy," she explained. "But I can pay you with this."

Dodge's eyes widened when he saw the blueberries.

He knew how hard Hattie had worked to pick and then can them. Plus it was a whole quart.

"No, no," Mr. Carlbom said. "That's much too much."

But Hattie knew she'd be in trouble if she didn't pay, so she stood firm.

"Well, all right," Mr. Carlbom finally agreed. "But only if I can fill another sack for you."

Hattie nodded, and he took a small paper bag from a stack on the counter and filled it with all kinds of hard candies. Dodge reached for the bag greedily, but stopped short when he saw Hattie's face.

Hattie didn't really want the candy, but she took it anyway. They were her blueberries and her last hope to earn some money this winter. Now she had only five jars left.

Wondering if she could sell the candy at school, Hattie retied Dodge's scarf around his neck and pulled his hat down over his forehead.

"It itches!" Dodge complained. Polly had recently made the hat from rough spun wool she'd gotten in a trade with a neighbor.

"A little itching is better than a head cold," Hattie reminded him. She pulled her own hat down and pushed open the door.

Looking around, Hattie was relieved to see that Lily was gone. She felt badly for yelling, but was still annoyed. Any sensible person should have realized that she was being a pest. Even a new girl.

31

Chapter Six

Hard Walk Home

Hattie led the way to the path out of town. The snow was hard so the walking was easy, if slippery.

"I'm sorry about the candy, Hat," Dodge said after a while. "I forgot the charity rule. And I didn't know it included candy. I hadn't had licorice bites in ages! I know it was dumb of me."

Hattie sighed. As frustrated as she was, she couldn't blame her little brother. He was only six. Who didn't want free candy?

Still, she was worried. She didn't know how she was going to explain the missing jar of berries. Selling them for money to keep Papa home was one thing. Trading them for candy was another. It would require some explaining. But she couldn't blame Dodge. She was the one who took the berries out of the larder in the first place.

"It's okay, Dodge. Just try to remember next time."

"I will, I promise," he said solemnly.

They walked past the Hayes farm on the outskirts of town. Two shaggy horses were munching on a small pile of hay. The wind was still gusty, and Hattie's shoulder was starting to ache.

"Let me carry one of those bags," Dodge offered.

Hattie shook her head. "No, thanks. I'm doing fine."

"I won't drop it!" Dodge insisted. "I'm good at carrying stuff. Aunt Polly lets me carry sacks of flour all the time."

"Quit pestering," Hattie scolded, panting a little. They were going up a hill.

Dodge didn't say anything else for a while, and Hattie tried to ignore the throbbing in her shoulder and the nagging worry in the back of her mind. She quickened her pace.

Almost everything she could see was white and gray. The white was the snow, covering the ground like a huge blanket. The gray was the sides of the giant barns and the tree trunks and bare branches that reached through the snow for the pale winter sky.

The only splashes of color were the occasional red barns or painted farmhouses, and the green fir trees that dotted the land.

As they passed a frozen pond Hattie stopped to catch her breath, laying her bags down gently on the ground. Dodge trudged up behind her. His head and arms hung low as if they weighed hundreds of pounds.

"Finally," Dodge panted from behind his scarf. "Is this a race or something?"

"I want to start on some presents," Hattie told him.

Really, she was hoping to get the blueberries back in the cellar before anyone noticed they were missing. She had to say something to Dodge, too.

"Don't tell anyone about the berries." Hattie looked at her brother as sternly as she could. "I'll give you another licorice bite when we get home if you promise to keep your mouth shut." She figured she could spare another piece. Aunt Polly always said you attract more flies with sugar than you do with vinegar.

Dodge grinned. He still had black goo on the corners of his mouth. "I can keep a secret," he promised. "Come on. Let's go!" He took the lead, bounding up the path. As Hattie hoisted the bags back over her shoulder and trudged after him, she wished she hadn't mentioned the candy. Now she'd be chasing after him!

"Hurry up, Hattie!" Dodge yelled over his shoulder.

"I'm coming," she shouted back. "Hold your horses a second. These bags are heavy!"

Dodge retraced his steps, running up to her. "Sorry," he panted. "Let me carry one. We'll get home faster."

Hattie hesitated. She wanted to carry them herself, to be safe. But she was tired. And she would still have chores to do when she got home. Besides, Dodge knew he'd already messed up today.

"Oh, all right," Hattie finally agreed. "But be careful!"

"Great!" Dodge crowed. He reached for the bag and grabbed a corner. As he stepped back, his foot landed on an icy section of the path. He slipped, the bag tipped, and one of the jars of blueberries fell out. It landed on the frozen ground and broke.

Horrified, Hattie watched the berries spill out, turning the white ice a bruised purply blue. She was so mad that she didn't move for five whole seconds. Then she let loose on her little brother.

"Dodge!" she yelled at the top of her lungs. "I told you to be careful! That's the second jar of blueberries you've wasted in two hours! Can't you do anything right? Do you *always* have to make *everything* worse?"

Hattie could see her breath disappearing into the cold winter air as Dodge stared back at her. He didn't say anything, but after a couple of seconds his bottom lip began to quiver. Then he turned around and hurried up the path toward home, leaving the second bag lying in the snow.

Hattie stood in the middle of the path, staring down at the blueberries. She probably could have salvaged some of them, but there were the pieces of glass to worry about. Besides, she didn't have any way to carry them, and there was no way she could get them in the house without Ruth and Polly finding out.

"Some hungry doe is going to be very happy when she finds this," she finally said with a sigh. She bent down and quickly picked out as much of the glass as she could, wrapping it in a piece of burlap ripped from one of the bags. Then she hefted both blueberry sacks — now a little lighter — over her shoulder and followed Dodge.

Hattie's nagging worry was now full-size. Four jars was a lot less than six. She hoped that it wouldn't be too noticeable on the shelf. She could picture Aunt Ruth with her hands on her hips asking what had happened. It wasn't like Hattie to sneak around. It wasn't like Hattie to yell at people, either, and she'd done that twice today.

Dodge trudged ahead of her on the trail, occasionally lifting a mitten to wipe his cheeks. Hattie knew he hadn't meant to drop the blueberries. He would never do anything like that on purpose. He'd only been trying to help. And it wasn't his fault that she'd taken the berries or that Lily Swenson had been spying on her in town. Watching him cry was only making Hattie feel worse.

Hattie hurried to catch up to her brother. Tapping him on the shoulder, she held out the lighter blueberry bag to him again. Dodge stopped and wiped the frozen tears from his face. Then he gave Hattie a sheepish look and took the bag — very, very carefully.

"Can I still have a licorice when we get home?" he asked quietly.

Hattie nodded and gave Dodge a weak smile. She could never stay mad at him for long.

As they rounded the last bend and the farmhouse

came into view, Hattie spotted a strange new car parked in front of the barn. Hattie's heart filled with joy at the sight of it. For the first time that day Hattie forgot all about the berries as she and Dodge raced up to the house.

Papa!

Chapter Seven
A Special Visit

"Papa! Papa!" Hattie whooped as she threw open the front door. But the man sitting at the kitchen table drinking a cup of coffee was not her father. In fact, Hattie had never seen this dark-haired stranger before in her life. Dressed in a fancy pin-striped suit, he was clearly not from anywhere around Iron Creek.

"Papa!" Dodge shouted, barreling through the door behind his sister a moment later. It only took a second for his face to fall, too.

"Oh, excuse me," Hattie said, feeling embarrassed.

"Well, now," the man said. "I always hate to be a disappointment. But even though I'm not your papa, I did bring someone along with me who I'm sure you'll be pleased to see." He winked a brown eye at Hattie and ran a hand over his slicked-back hair.

Just then two familiar laughs echoed from Aunt Polly's bedroom. One was Polly's, of course. And the other was Aunt Stella's!

Hattie dropped her coat on top of the berry sacks,

rushed down the hall after Dodge, and burst into Aunt Polly's room.

Aunt Stella was unpacking her suitcase, putting neatly ironed cotton blouses into a drawer.

"Aunt Stella!" Dodge and Hattie shouted together. There was a blur of arms and backs and heads as they greeted their third aunt with a hug worth about a hundred.

"Mmmmmm, those are the best hugs I've had in ages," Stella said with a laugh. "I ought to come here more often."

Dodge unwrapped his arms from Aunt Stella's waist. "Have you seen the world yet?" he asked. "What does it look like?"

"I haven't seen the half of it," Stella confessed as she tousled his hair. "But what I've seen is big and wide."

Dodge looked thoughtful. "That sounds just like Wisconsin."

"Except for the city lights," she agreed.

The man from the kitchen poked his head in the bedroom and Hattie and Dodge were officially introduced to Stella's boyfriend, Bo Chance. Even though he wasn't Papa, Hattie liked Bo right away. He had a deep rolling laugh and twinkly eyes. And he seemed just crazy about Aunt Stella.

Hattie hated to tear herself away — there was so much to talk about and so many stories to listen to —

but she said she needed to start on her barn chores and slipped into the kitchen to get the berries and put them back on their shelf in the cellar. She pushed them together and spread them out, trying to figure out which way they looked like more. Either way it looked two jars short.

Hattie held her left thumb and made a quick wish that nobody would notice. Then she headed out to the barn. She broke the ice, mucked out the stalls, fed the animals, and gathered the few laid eggs before dashing back into the toasty farmhouse.

Hattie stepped into the front hall and unbuttoned her wool coat. Aunt Ruth had come in while Hattie was out, and Hattie could hear her telling Stella how hard everyone had been working while she'd been gone.

Polly was starting supper and Hattie pumped some water and put it on the stove to heat for washing dishes later. Then she filled everyone's water glasses while Dodge set the table. When everything was ready they all sat down to bowls of steaming hot soup and a basket of warm biscuits.

As Hattie looked around the table, she realized that her terrible day was not so terrible anymore.

The next day was even better. In the morning, Bo declared that it was no trouble to get his car started and drive everyone to church.

"Nonsense," Aunt Ruth said. "We'll take the buckboard like we usually do." Aunt Ruth thought cars were useless in winter. She always drained theirs as soon as the season's first cold snap hit, which was usually well before Thanksgiving. She said it was the practical thing to do.

Luckily, Aunt Polly convinced Ruth that a ride to church would be fun. So everyone piled on their coats and hats and mittens, and they all squeezed into Bo's shiny new DeSoto.

Bo's car was nothing like the Ecklunds' '26 Dodge. It was dark green, shiny, and roomy. Plus it had heat, a roof, and a glass windshield!

Bo let Dodge honk the horn as they lurched forward and bounced over the wagon ruts.

"Like I said, ridiculous," Ruth grumbled from her spot in the backseat. But Dodge was having the time of his life, whooping and hollering the whole way. And Hattie was convinced that any amount of jostling was worth pulling up in front of the church in such style. Bo's car was as fancy as any car in Duluth and Aunt Stella looked as fine as any city woman, with her French organdy dress and her long, wavy hair pinned on the side. That new girl didn't have a thing on Aunt Stella.

When they got home after church, Hattie, Aunt Polly, and Aunt Stella spent the rest of the morning in the kitchen, cooking up the biggest Sunday dinner they'd had in weeks.

Aunt Polly baked three loaves of her wonderful

whole wheat bread — and even used a little bit of molasses to sweeten it up.

Aunt Ruth brought in two fresh rabbits from the smokehouse, and Aunt Stella coated them with a little bacon grease, cornmeal, and salt and pepper before putting them to roast in the oven.

Hattie peeled the carrots and got them ready to go in the roasting pan. Then she made her specialty: stretch potatoes. She carefully sliced two onions and a heap of lightly boiled potatoes. She layered them in a casserole and sprinkled them with leftover brown bread she'd soaked and pulled into pieces. Then she put the whole thing in the oven.

By the time they sat down, the house smelled as good as it did on a holiday.

Stella and Bo entertained everyone at the table with stories of their adventures in Minneapolis and Chicago. They'd been to nightclubs and heard all kinds of music, like jazz and swing, and Bo said he'd even seen the famous musician Tommy Dorsey! His swing band was one of Aunt Polly's favorites. She and Hattie loved to dance around the living room when they heard him on the radio.

Everyone was impressed — except Aunt Ruth. She didn't say anything out loud, but the look on her face told Hattie that she didn't approve of her little sister's adventures. They were *not* practical.

In spite of Ruth's disapproving looks, it was a wonderful dinner — and Bo and Aunt Stella announced that they were going to stay until after Christmas!

"Yippee!" Dodge yelled. Hattie agreed. Things always seemed a little more exciting when Aunt Stella was around.

After the table was cleaned and the dishes done, Bo cleared his throat loudly.

"Such a fine meal definitely deserves a fine finish, so we should all go into town to have pie and coffee — or maybe," he added, giving Hattie a grin, "hot chocolate?"

"Yippee!" Dodge yelled again, and everyone but Ruth was convinced. However, she *did* say that she and Abe and Frank would take care of the barn chores while Hattie and Dodge were gone.

"But only for this afternoon," Ruth added, sounding more like her stern self.

Thrilled, Hattie gave her a giant hug. Aunt Ruth almost *never* let her out of chores.

For the first time in ages, Hattie forgot her troubles. As she snuggled between Aunt Polly and Aunt Stella in the backseat of Bo's DeSoto, as she bit into her very own slice of blueberry pie, as she laughed at another of Bo's crazy stories, she felt happy. Neither Bo nor Aunt Stella were Papa, and Aunt Ruth might think they were extravagant, but Christmas with them would be a holiday to remember.

Chapter Eight
Stella Stirs It Up

Hattie woke the next morning to the smell of coffee and the sound of voices in the kitchen. Bo must have brought the wood in for Aunt Polly. Hattie dressed quickly, anxious to get through her barn chores and have a minute to sit with Aunt Stella and Bo before school.

In the kitchen, Polly was bent over the stove. Bo sat with his feet on the table, both hands wrapped around a steaming cup. Ruth stomped her boots as she came in the door with a load of wood.

Hattie dashed by them all — aiming to get her coat and get going — but Bo caught her around the waist.

"Hold on there, Missy," he laughed. "Where you running off to? You haven't had your breakfast or said good morning to your Uncle Bo!"

Hattie pulled free, giggling, and started to explain. Aunt Ruth interrupted.

"The girl has chores to do before school, Mr. Chance," she said as she noisily dumped a load of chopped wood

44

by the stove. "Maybe you haven't noticed, but everyone works on this farm."

Bo was unfazed by Ruth's no-nonsense tone. "Surely the little lady can take one day off to see her aunty," he chided, poking Hattie in the ribs.

Hattie's giggle was cut short.

"She had yesterday afternoon off, if you'll remember," Ruth replied even more icily. "But that's it. Livestock doesn't take a vacation and neither do we. If you'll be staying on I'll have to ask you to kindly stay out of family business."

This time Bo stopped joking. His smile faded and he looked a little like a sick calf. Slowly he swung his feet off the table, working his tongue around his mouth as if he was searching in there for the right thing to say. Hattie knew just how he felt.

"Ruthie, what in the world are you scolding Bo for!" Stella said, sweeping in from Aunt Polly's bedroom, still taking pins from her hair. "And what's this about Bo not being family?"

Stella had come in with a smile and a teasing tone, but the smile faded as she caught Ruth's gaze. Soon the two were glaring at each other over Hattie and Bo's heads.

Hattie wanted to crawl under the table, but felt a little too afraid to move. She didn't want to call attention to herself and catch any of Aunt Ruth's wrath. The best thing to do would be to get out of the kitchen and on to her chores. As quietly as she could, she pulled on her boots, took her coat off the hook, and slipped out the door.

Before the latch clicked shut behind her she heard Ruth growl, "Just because you're slumming with this fancy-pants does not make him family."

Poor Bo did not know what he was in for.

Now, instead of rushing through her chores, Hattie found herself lingering in the barn.

"Even you aren't as cranky as Aunt Ruth," she told Rusty as he pecked at her boot laces. In the warm glow of the previous day, Hattie had almost forgotten that Aunt Stella and Aunt Ruth couldn't be in the same house for too long before they started going at it like barn cats.

Ruth had never approved of Stella's leaving the farm, calling her a flibbertigibbet and a dream-chaser. Ruth always said that Stella would be back one day — to stay. She never liked any of Stella's beaux and kept telling her little sister to settle down and marry a farmer, or at least a logging man.

But everyone knew that Stella wasn't happy on the farm. She'd told Hattie she'd been dreaming of making it to the big cities since she was a little girl. Even at Hattie's age she was longing for bigger places — cities with grand theaters and electric streetlights.

Aunt Polly had told Hattie how, when Stella was little, she'd dress up the barn cats and chickens in costumes she'd made. She'd even try to get the animals to participate in stage shows!

Four years ago, when she was just sixteen, Stella had set off to see the world for herself. It was hard to travel and do what she wanted with the little money she made working lunch counters. But Stella was not discouraged. She knew dreams didn't come true overnight.

Hattie sighed as she finished grooming the horses and put the curry comb back into the storage bucket. If only her aunts could just get along until Christmas!

Hattie was about to open the kitchen door when Bo came barreling out, almost bowling her over. Dodge was right on his heels, carrying Hattie's lunch and books.

"How about a ride to school?" Bo asked Hattie, buttoning up his cashmere coat. His smile had lost a little of its sparkle.

"Sure." Hattie tried to return the grin. She knew Aunt Ruth wouldn't be happy that they were riding in Bo's car again, but she didn't think Aunt Ruth would be happy about much right now.

"Here, Hat," Dodge said. He handed over her things and some biscuits wrapped up in a napkin. "I brought your stuff. I don't think you want to go in there."

Hattie followed Dodge and Bo to the car. She sat glumly on the front seat while Bo filled the radiator and Dodge pointed at each engine part, asking Bo what it did. You'd have thought they didn't have a car of their own.

When the car was finally running, Hattie sat back and tried to eat a biscuit. It was stone-cold. With a sigh, Hattie wrapped it back up. She didn't feel very hungry anyway.

Dodge sat next to Bo in the front, yammering on. Hattie wondered how he got over the aunts fighting so quickly. Dodge bounced back up from things like a rubber ball. Sometimes it made Hattie jealous.

"Are you really going to New York City?" Dodge yelled over the engine noise.

"That's right!" Bo replied. He had one hand on the steering wheel and one hand on his hat. "We're headed to the Big Apple. And if things work out, your Aunt Stella is going to be a big star." Bo's grin widened and his sparkle returned when he talked about Stella.

Even Hattie didn't doubt Aunt Stella would be a star. She was as pretty as any of the girls Hattie had seen in magazines — or even the movies — and loads more fun.

While the boys chatted on about New York, Hattie started to feel a little better. Maybe the fight would blow over by the afternoon. Maybe Christmas would still be saved. And maybe Lily would see her drive up to school in a new DeSoto and hear all about her aunt heading to New York City — a city that made Duluth look smaller than Iron Creek.

Lily was outside to see the Best kids pull up in Bo's

shiny car, all right. As soon as she saw who was inside she turned on her heel and hurried into the schoolhouse.

She's just a snob, Hattie thought as she climbed out of the car. But in the back of her mind, Hattie wasn't completely convinced.

Thanks to Dodge, all of the kids knew about Aunt Stella and her big plans by recess. Instead of swarming around Lily, everyone was packed around Hattie. They were full of questions.

"Can she really get work as an actress?" Jenny Soma wanted to know.

"Is it true she thinks Minneapolis is too small?" Karin Withers asked.

"Where'd her boyfriend get the money to buy that car?" Billy Sanders piped up.

Everyone had so many questions that Hattie had to write them down to remember them all.

"I'll ask her tonight," she told her friends. "I promise I'll find out everything."

On the walk home Dodge danced circles around Hattie as she slid her feet over the icy ground.

"Maybe I can go with them," Dodge thought aloud. "Maybe I can be a star, too."

Hattie just laughed. She didn't want to burst his bubble. And it was fun to think of Stella making it big — of watching her very own aunt on a movie screen! Still, deep down, something was spoiling Hattie's daydream. She could still hear Ruth and Stella's angry voices shouting back and forth in her head.

When they rounded the bend, Bo's car was nowhere to be seen.

"Maybe it's in the barn," Dodge said.

"Maybe," Hattie said.

As soon as they entered the kitchen, Hattie knew the car wasn't in the barn. Aunt Polly was knitting by the radio, but otherwise the house was quiet.

"Is Aunt Stella in town?" Hattie asked, holding her thumb. "Did they go in for pie?"

Polly got up from her chair. "I'm sorry, Sugar," she said, wrapping her arms around her niece and nephew. "They decided they needed to head to New York early. They wanted me to tell you both Merry Christmas."

"Hmmph," Hattie shrugged out of her aunt's hug. She didn't want Aunt Polly to know how upset she was.

Alone in her room, Hattie blinked back tears. She took the list of questions for Aunt Stella out of her pocket and put it with the letters from Papa. Maybe she'd get to ask her questions someday. And maybe someday Papa would come home.

Hattie squeezed her eyes closed. Right now she could only hope.

Chapter Nine
The Perfect Tree

"Hey kids," said the voice on the radio, "anybody know how many days until Christmas?"

"Four!" the audience shouted.

"So don't you think it's time to 'Deck the Halls'?" The announcer was leading in to Aunt Polly's favorite Christmas carol.

Polly hummed along quietly as she finished the breakfast dishes. It was the most Christmas spirit there'd been in the house since Stella had left the week before. Polly hummed a little louder on the second verse and pretty soon Dodge joined in on the "fa-la-las." Hattie listened as she swept the floor, but she still did not feel even a little bit Christmassy.

How could they be cheery when everything was so horribly wrong? Stella and Bo were gone. They hadn't heard a word from Papa. Hattie's moneymaking plan had failed and she hadn't had any time to work on a new one. She hadn't even started on Christmas presents for her aunts.

"How would you elves like to help me bake some Christmas cookies?" Polly suggested.

Hattie felt more like Scrooge than an elf, but she knew Aunt Polly was just trying to cheer her up.

"I think I've saved just enough sugar to make your favorite," Polly coaxed. She took the sugar jar down from its high shelf and put it on the table next to the flour.

"Woo-hoo!" Dodge yelped. He grabbed the broom away from Hattie and galloped with it around the kitchen like the Lone Ranger.

Hattie took the recipe card from her aunt. It was written in her mama's handwriting: *Ethel's Sugar Cookies*.

Hattie remembered helping make these same cookies the last Christmas Mama was alive. She had been about Dodge's age, and Mama had let her mash up the butter with a fork before they put the sugar in the bowl.

Now Aunt Polly put a bowl in front of Hattie, and Dodge galloped up with the butter. Hattie measured out a full cup of sugar, being careful not to spill any. Sugar was one of the hardest things to come by these days. She was just about to tip the cup in when Dodge hit her hand with his broom horse and the white crystals scattered everywhere.

"Oh!" Polly cried. Her hands flew to her face as the broom smacked down on the floor. Hattie and Dodge stood stock-still with their mouths wide open.

"I . . . I . . ." Dodge stammered.

"Out," said Polly quietly. "I think you should both go out."

"I'm sorry," Dodge whispered.

"I know," Polly said.

"I could sweep most of it up, it might be okay..." Hattie offered.

"You kids just go play," Polly said in a quiet voice that was somehow worse than Ruth's booming one. Polly didn't move as Hattie helped Dodge with his coat. She was standing in the same place with her hands on her face when Hattie closed the front door.

Outside, Hattie whirled on her brother. But one look at his face told her she couldn't be mad. Dodge was just a kid. He was just a kid trying to have a good Christmas. Instead of scolding, Hattie buttoned the top button of his coat. She looked around at the new snow that had fallen overnight — enough to soften all the edges and make everything fresh and white. At least it *looked* like Christmas.

"C'mon, Tonto," Hattie said. "Let's go see what Frank and Abe are up to."

They didn't have to go far. Before they got to the bunkhouse they found Frank hitching the horses up to the buckboard.

"I was just fixin' to find you two," he said when he saw them. "How about we pull that pretty aunt of yours out of the kitchen and go for a ride in the snow?"

Hattie figured it was best to leave Aunt Polly alone for awhile so she told Frank she was busy.

"You're supposed to keep out from underfoot, is that it?" he asked.

"Something like that," Hattie nodded.

"Well, then, I guess we'll have to find the perfect Christmas tree on our own and surprise her," Frank said with a slow smile.

Dodge was in the buckboard before Frank could even turn around. Hattie felt grateful, if only for her brother's sake. Maybe they could spare a little Christmas fun for him.

As they headed for the woods Hattie noticed a column of smoke rising from the work shed chimney. Aunt Ruth had been spending a lot of time in there, something she did when she and Polly had a fight.

Hattie hadn't heard them fighting, but she thought maybe Polly blamed Ruth for causing Stella to leave so early. Letting out a heavy sigh, Hattie watched her breath disappear into the cold air. It was bad enough that Stella was gone. Having Ruth and Polly fight about it would make it even worse.

Up front, Dodge and Frank suddenly stopped talking to watch a winter deer in the woods. It was a young stag with a small rack of fuzzy horns. His white tail fluttered up and down as he dashed deeper into the forest.

When they got to an area with lots of young saplings,

Frank stopped the buckboard. They all hopped down to search for the perfect tree. The snowfall the night before had left the evergreens sparkling and heavy with snow.

Ahead of them, two jackrabbits bounded almost invisibly through the powdery white. The hares looked like they were having fun and Hattie began to feel the tightness in her chest loosen. With a whoop she bounded after them, grabbing snow in her mittens as she went. It felt good to be out in the woods.

Dodge threw the first snowball, but Hattie was ready. She returned fire. Then Frank joined in the fun and she was hit from two directions at once. Hattie crumpled in the snow, her hands clutched to her chest. She rolled over for a last melodramatic breath — and spotted the perfect tree!

"Time out," Hattie called. "Look." She pointed as best she could with mittens on.

"By golly," Frank hollered, "I think you found us a tree."

Dodge started singing "O Tannenbaum" and marched around the beautiful balsam fir. The tree was already decorated with snow, icicles, and a few forgotten fall leaves. It looked so pretty it seemed a shame to shake it off.

"Timber!" Dodge called as Frank swung the ax for the last time. The tree fell softly in the snow and the three dragged it back to the wagon. With the smell of fir in her nose and Dodge singing off-key carols at the top of his lungs, Hattie couldn't help but feel a whole lot better.

Taking a deep breath, she piped up and sang along in her merriest Christmas voice.

Chapter Ten

A Christmas Angel

When they got home, Hattie and Dodge pulled the tree off the wagon, and Frank carried it into the house.

"Surprise!" Dodge yelled as they stampeded through the door.

Hattie was relieved to see Polly's smile when she spotted the tree. She felt even better when she saw a small batch of cookies cooling on the kitchen counter.

"Oh, kids, it's beautiful!" Aunt Polly declared, circling the little fir. "The prettiest one we've had in years. Let me get the stand and the blanket, and we can put it up right away."

She hurried out of the kitchen, and Hattie could hear her digging around in the hall closet. A moment later she came back with a green cast-iron Christmas tree stand. She placed it on the floor, and Frank brought in a bucket full of snow. He put it by the stove to melt so they could give it to the tree later. Then Frank trimmed off the lowest branches and secured the tree in the stand. Dodge wrapped the red wool blanket around to hide the bottom.

Everyone stood back to admire the tree. It was the tallest one they'd had in a long time, nearly brushing the ceiling.

"It's perfect!" Dodge declared.

"It certainly is," came a voice from behind them. It was Aunt Ruth, who had just come in from the barn. She smiled at everyone as she pulled off her snowy hat and gloves. If she and Polly were fighting, Hattie certainly couldn't tell.

Aunt Polly flashed Frank a warm smile. "Thank you," she said.

"Hattie here found it," Frank told her. "And right in the middle of a snowball fight, too!"

"You three had a snowball fight without me?" Aunt Ruth sounded put out.

"Yup," Dodge said. "We aced her."

"They got me good," Hattie admitted.

"Well, don't you worry, Hat," Ruth replied as she put an arm around her niece. "It'll be an even match next time."

Hattie smiled. Her Aunt Ruth might be practical, but she *always* had time for a good snowball fight.

"Who wants tea and cookies?" Aunt Polly piped up. "I've got some fresh from the oven. And then I think that tree will be needing some ornaments — and popcorn strings, too."

Frank insisted he had chores to do and headed out to unhitch the team. But everyone else hurried to the kitchen. The water was already hot, so Hattie got out the tea — red clover and fennel that Aunt Polly had gathered and dried in the summer — while Dodge got the mugs.

Dodge gobbled up his cookie before his tea was even cool enough to drink, but Hattie savored hers. She knew there wasn't enough sugar to make another batch, and the cookie was baked to a perfect golden brown.

"I'm gonna make some snowflakes," Dodge announced, thumping his tea mug down on the table.

"*Going to*," Aunt Polly gently corrected.

Dodge shrugged and bounded up from the table — practically knocking over the mug he'd just put down. Then he got out the wrapping paper Polly had saved and ironed from last year. Soon he was folding and cutting away, his tongue sticking out of the corner of his mouth. It reminded Hattie of her papa, who did the very same thing whenever he was concentrating hard.

Dodge's cuts were squiggly and his snowflakes were all lopsided, but Aunt Polly said they were lovely.

"We'd better be getting those popcorn strings on that tree," Aunt Ruth said, shoving back her chair.

Aunt Polly had already gotten out the paper ornament box, the one with the faded red-and-green lining. Ruth pulled off the lid and lifted out the popcorn strings. Every year after Christmas the box was carefully repacked with the popcorn strings on top, since they were the first decoration to go up.

While Bing Crosby crooned on the radio, everyone helped decorate the tree. First Ruth draped the popcorn strings all the way around, from the top to the bottom. Then Hattie added pinecones and hollow walnuts tied with bright red ribbon. Polly carefully placed each of her six glass balls in a special spot. Then she clipped a dozen small candleholders to the limbs, making sure they were straight and wouldn't burn any other boughs. Dodge completed the job with his paper snowflakes.

"It's gorgeous," Polly said with a happy smile.

"But it needs something. . . ." Ruth shook her head and crinkled her forehead as she looked the tree over. "I just can't figure out what it could be."

"The angel!" Dodge shouted. "The angel!"

Ruth let out a relieved sigh. "Of course," she said, stretching out the sounds of the letters, "the *angel*."

Hattie pulled another, smaller box from inside the ornament one. Taking off the lid, she unwrapped several sheets of crinkled paper — until a beautiful glass angel sat in her lap.

The angel had been Mama's, a gift from Papa on their first Christmas together. Now that Mama was gone, the angel had become part of the aunts' ornament collection. It was clear glass crystal, and the angel had her hands out like she was flying. Hattie liked to think of Mama like that — an angel flying through heaven.

Ruth lifted Dodge up on her shoulders and he placed

the angel on the very top of the tree. There was just enough space for her below the ceiling, and she smiled lovingly down at everyone in the room.

Maybe she'll make Christmas turn out all right, Hattie thought as she looked up at the angel. *Maybe the angel will make Papa come home to stay.*

After the tree-decorating, everyone got their chores done so they could linger over supper and breathe in the wonderful Christmassy smell the tree spread throughout the farmhouse. Polly cooked a delicious stew, and everyone seemed to be in a good mood at last. The empty spaces left from Aunt Stella and Bo's leaving were finally beginning to fill in.

Hattie felt content to just gaze down the hall at the tree in the living room, and only half-listened to the dinner conversation.

"I ran into Mr. Swenson at the feed store," Frank said between bites, "and he seemed all mixed up about what to buy. Does he know much about north country farming?"

Aunt Ruth shook her head. "Not much, I'm afraid. I was over there last week to see if they needed help choosing spring seeds, and he said no, even though I could tell he did. I guess some men don't like taking advice from women."

"Well, he'd be wise to listen to what you have to say,

Ruth," Abe replied. "You've been farming this country for near twenty years. There isn't a man around who knows farming better than you."

Ruth smiled at the compliment.

Just then the talk was interrupted by a knock on the door. Frank got up and opened it, ushering two stern men into the room. They wore city suits, but the elbows and cuffs were threadbare.

It was the Lofstrom brothers.

"Evening," Frederik, the taller brother, said, tipping his hat but not bothering to remove it completely. His Nordic accent was strong and his nose twitched when he talked. "I'm sure you know why we're here."

"We've come to collect our due on the tractor loan," Wendel, the shorter, pudgier brother spoke up. His round face made his eyes look small. "You're five months overdue, and we've been mighty patient with you this far. Now I'm afraid our patience has run out."

Aunt Polly's eyes widened, but just for a second. She pulled herself together and briskly began to clear the dishes from the table. Hattie helped her. Out of the corner of her eye, she could see Ruth standing between the table and the Lofstroms.

"Come on, boys," Aunt Ruth said. "You know darn well that everyone has been hit with hard times. We're working ourselves to the bone just to feed our family. There isn't enough to pay the tractor loan."

"I'm afraid we're not leaving until we get some good money from you," Wendel Lofstrom said.

Ruth planted her hands on her hips, making her shoulders look even broader than they were. Hattie knew the stance well.

"Don't you try playing hardball with me, Wendel Lofstrom," Aunt Ruth growled. "I've known you since you were toddling around your mama's house wearing diapers, which we all know you did for much too long."

Hattie winced. Now Wendel Lofstrom was probably mad, on top of wanting his money.

Aunt Polly cleared her throat and stepped forward. "Can I interest you two gentlemen in a nice cup of coffee and some Christmas cookies? We were just about to have some ourselves, and would be pleased to have you join us."

Ruth smiled stiffly and gestured to the table. "Please," she said through gritted teeth, "have a seat."

The Lofstroms sat down and Hattie watched Aunt Polly place more than a dozen of her wonderful cookies on the table. Hattie almost cried out. How could Aunt Polly feed their precious Christmas cookies to the Lofstroms?

The Lofstroms each took a cookie and bit into it. Hattie could tell by their expressions that they thought the cookies were delicious, but they didn't say anything. In fact, they didn't say a single word the entire time they

sat at the kitchen table. They just ate the cookies —
four apiece — and drank their coffee in silence. Finally,
after the longest fifteen minutes of Hattie's life, they
got up.

"No need to see us out," Wendel said. The two men
walked out the door, letting it slam behind them.

Aunt Polly let out a relieved sigh, and everyone re-
laxed a little. But the festive Christmas mood was gone
again.

The Lofstroms would be back.

Chapter Eleven
The Jungle

On the ride home after church on Sunday, Aunt Polly told Hattie and Dodge that she had a surprise for them. Hattie guessed what it was right away: a letter from Papa.

She was right. This one was dated only six days earlier. Dodge opened the letter and handed it to Hattie to read aloud.

December 16, 1934
Salt Lake City, Utah

Dear Dodge and Hattie,
I'm writing to you from the land of the Great Salt Lake in Utah, a land as strange as any I've seen. Salt Lake City itself is big and bustling, with the Wasach Mountains springing up on the east side. There's a giant temple here built by a religious group called the Mormons. They seem to be nice folks who stick together and help one another as best they can during these tough times.

The Best Christmas

To the west is a giant salt lake, which is where the city gets its name. It's unusual for a lake to be filled with salt water, and people here are as proud of that lake as they are of anything else.

Farther west is the Great Salt Lake Desert. It's flat as a pancake, a dry salt lake bed. That salty sand goes on and on as far as you can see and makes a man who's used to trees and rolling hills a little uncomfortable.

Work here is a tiny bit better than most places. Copper mining is a big industry, and some of the mines are still working. Some folks seem to have a few extra coins to buy this and that. So I'm sending along two dollars for your aunts. I'd like to tell you kids to use it for Christmas, but seeing as I'm not there I can't decide the best way to use this little bit of money. I'll bet the farm needs it most.

By the time you get this it will be almost Christmas. I long to be home in Wisconsin with you, but I can't make promises I might not be able to keep. Please know that I will do my best. Even if I don't make it, I will be there in spirit, giving you hugs and kisses, getting in Aunt Ruth's way, and gobbling up Aunt Polly's delicious Christmas dinner.

Please behave yourselves and mind your aunts.

I know they're taking as good care of you two as I ever could.

Love and hugs to you both,
Papa

"He sent us two whole dollars!" Dodge said, waving the bills in the air. "Now we can pay the Lofstroms!"

Aunt Polly wiped her hands on her apron and took the money. "We certainly can," she agreed. "That will help quite a bit around here."

Hattie knew that Aunt Polly was just being her positive self. Two dollars was not much at all when they were months and months overdue on their loan. But Dodge didn't need to know that.

Polly tucked the bills into a tin can and put it on the shelf above the stove. The aunts hadn't kept their money in a bank since the bank panic had happened. They'd had nearly fifty dollars in an account when the banks had closed. When they'd opened thirty days later, they could only get five dollars out. The rest was gone for good.

Hattie refolded the letter and put it back in the envelope. *Salt Lake City*, she said in her head, *Salt Lake City*. She tried to picture the giant map of the United States on the wall at school, but she couldn't quite remember where Salt Lake City was. Besides far away, that is.

The Best Christmas

Tucking the letter into her pocket, Hattie went into the living room and pulled the old United States atlas off the bookshelf. She flipped to the page with all the states on it, and found Utah. It was next to Nevada, only two states away from California, and three big states away from Wisconsin. Papa would still have to travel north after he got far enough east.

Hattie slammed the book shut with a sigh. How long did it take to get from Salt Lake City to Wisconsin on the trains? She had no idea and knew that her aunts wouldn't, either.

Hattie sat with the book on her lap for a few minutes, thinking. Then her eyes widened.

She knew exactly who to ask.

After Sunday dinner, Hattie managed to sneak away by herself. She felt a little guilty for not asking permission to go, but she didn't want to lie. If she'd told her aunts where she was going, they probably would have made her turn the compost pile all afternoon to keep her busy.

Hattie hurried along the path to town. It was a little warmer today, and there was no wind. Before long she was loosening the scarf around her neck to cool off.

Hattie made it to town in record time and headed for the river. She was going to "The Jungle," the tent-town hobo camp. It was where men who couldn't get in at

Dolph Peterson's lived. Dolph let men swamp out the tavern in exchange for a cot upstairs and a blue plate supper. It was the cheapest meal and roof you could come by in Iron Creek.

Hattie had never been to the Jungle before, but she'd heard all kinds of stories about it. In the summer lots of the kids hung around the Jungle and even fished with the hobos. It was no accident that their camp was set at the best fishing hole in the river.

Some adults in town told stories and said that hobos were dangerous criminals on the run from the law. But Aunt Ruth said they were people like Papa who were on the road because of the Depression, trying to earn a little money. There were also a few misfits and wanderers living in the Jungle — people who didn't quite fit in where they were, or people itchin' to travel, like Aunt Stella. As a rule, hobos didn't steal.

The hobo traffic rode the rails — jumping in boxcars without tickets — traveling from town to town and state to state looking for work and meals and a place to belong. They worked for every crust of bread they got. "For the most part they're honest men fallen on hard times," Ruth always said.

As Hattie neared the shabby-looking camp, she hoped her Aunt Ruth was right. Her heart pounded in her chest as she made her way toward three men standing around a fire in an empty oil barrel.

"Well, what've we here?" one of the men said as he looked Hattie over. He wore a tattered gray coat that was missing most of its buttons, and his cheeks were covered in black stubble. "Are you lost, or maybe looking for someone?"

Hattie tried to speak, but her voice cracked and no words came out.

"Speak up, Miss," said a taller hobo in a brown coat. At least it *looked* brown. Maybe that was just dirt. "We don't bite. Not unless we're *real* hungry." The man smiled at Hattie, and she saw that he was missing a front tooth.

"Come on, there, Bertie," piped up the third hobo by the fire. He had lots of freckles and a few strands of greasy red hair stuck out from under his hat. "You're scaring the girl."

"I was only teasing, Red," Bertie replied with his missing-tooth grin.

Hattie steeled her nerves and stepped forward. "Afternoon," she greeted. "My name is Hattie Best, and I was wondering if you gentlemen could answer a question for me."

The three hobos looked at Hattie with amused smiles. She guessed that little girls from town didn't often visit the Jungle. But she was here for a reason, and it was important. So she went on.

"My papa is in Salt Lake City. Or he was about a week

ago. I was wondering, do you think he could make it home by Christmas if he was riding the rails?"

The hobos exchanged glances, and the man with the red hair smiled down at Hattie.

"Well, now, let's see," the hobo with the missing buttons said. "Salt Lake City, Utah, to Iron Creek, Wisconsin. In how long, you say?"

Hattie counted the days in her head for the hundredth time, just to be sure her information was correct. There were three days to Christmas and the letter was posted six days ago. If she took off the day that Papa mailed the letter, then that gave him — "Eight days," she said.

"Eight days, eight days," the hobo repeated. "Seems to me I made a trip from Salt Lake to Chicago in six days once. Now, of course, Chicago is farther east, but not as far north. And it's a direct shot, no transferin' trains. Still and all, I'd say it was possible."

He held his hands out over the fire, and Hattie saw that his gloves only half-covered his fingers. The ends of his fingers were raw and chapped. "Whaddaya think, boys?"

The man in the brown coat, Bertie, nodded. "For sure possible, Odie," he agreed, "as long as the weather holds. A storm can stop the trains from runnin' lickety-split."

"True." Red nodded. "But if he's got you here waitin'

for him, I'm sure he'll make it home if it can be done."
He winked, and Hattie was suddenly filled with hope.

"Now, why don't you warm those hands of yours?"
said Odie, the first hobo. "We can make a little room
around the fire, can't we boys?"

The three men crowded together on one side of the
barrel to make room for Hattie. She stepped forward,
and the heat from the fire spread warmth through her
hands and across her face. After a few minutes she felt
positively toasty. Papa would make it home for Christmas, she was sure of it.

Hattie wanted to stand by the fire a while listening to
the men talk, but she had a long walk home and didn't
want to be late.

"I'd best be getting home. There's not much daylight
left," she finally said. "Thanks so much for answering
my question."

"Do you want us to walk you?" the red-haired man
offered.

Hattie smiled. She liked this hobo and imagined he
had a family of his own somewhere. Maybe he was traveling around trying to earn money, just like Papa.

"No, thanks," she finally said, not wanting the man to
have to leave the warmth of the fire. "I know my way
and I'm a fast walker."

"I believe you are, Hattie Best," the hobo replied with
a nod. "I believe you are."

Bertie pointed to a path leading through the Jungle in

a different direction from where Hattie came in. "That's the fastest way to town," he explained. "It'll put you right on Main Street."

Hattie nodded and waved good-bye. "Thanks again," she called as she started up the path. She made her way past other fires and groups of hobos. Some were eating from tin cans, and others were smoking cigarettes. A couple of them noticed Hattie and looked up. But they didn't make her nervous anymore.

As she passed the last fire, Hattie couldn't help but overhear the name Swenson. She slowed down to listen. It seemed a couple of hobos had been out to her new neighbors' farm to try and get some work in exchange for food.

"They had plenty of work," Hattie heard someone say, "but nothing to pay for the help. The smokehouse was empty."

Hattie thought of her own smokehouse, which Abe and Aunt Ruth kept stocked all winter. Their root cellar had plenty of food, too — even now, almost halfway through the cold months. The Swensons moved to town too late to have a harvest, and probably didn't bring much from Duluth. If they were low on food now, how would they make it through until spring?

With a pang of guilt, Hattie realized that the Swensons wouldn't have much to eat on their Christmas table.

Hattie hurried across Main Street, past the Hayes

farm. The winter sun sank lower in the sky, and the temperature began to drop. Hattie tightened her scarf around her neck and pulled her hat down over her ears.

All the way home, Hattie's mind flipped back and forth between the two things she'd learned at the Jungle: Papa could make it home for Christmas, and the Swensons were bad off in terms of food for the winter. One filled her heart with hope, and the other made her feel sick to her stomach.

By the time Hattie was heading up her own road, her mind was reeling and her toes were numb. She pushed open the front door, relieved to get out of the cold . . . until she saw Aunt Ruth standing in the hallway with her hands on her hips. Behind her, Dodge sat at the kitchen table, his eyes wide.

"Harriet Elizabeth Best," Ruth boomed out in her I-mean-business voice. Her eyes bore into Hattie's like Rusty's beak on bare feet. "Just where do you think you've been?"

Chapter Twelve

Secrets

Hattie knew she shouldn't have gone off without telling anyone where she was, but she didn't know Aunt Ruth would be middle-name mad.

"I —" she stammered.

"Out with it, Harriet," Ruth barked again. "Where did you have to go that was so important you made your Aunt Polly sick with worry?"

Polly lowered her eyebrows and gave Hattie a stern look over Ruth's shoulder, but it was gone in an instant. Hattie got the feeling that Polly wasn't the one who'd been worried sick.

"I can't really say," Hattie muttered into her wool scarf.

"You can't say?" Ruth repeated, taking a step back. "You can't say? Well, maybe you can't —"

"Now Ruth," Polly put her hand on her sister's shoulder. "Remember what season it is. I haven't been asking you to explain why you're spending so much time in that work shed."

Ruth was quiet a moment. Then her face softened.

"You could have told us when you'd be back!" she said with a final fierce glance at Hattie.

Hattie sighed a huge sigh of relief. All things considered, she'd gotten off easy. *Thank goodness for Aunt Polly*, she thought as she unwrapped her scarf. *She knows how to soften Ruth's wallop better than anyone.*

Hattie was about to give Polly a big hug when she realized that now both aunts were turned back around and facing Dodge, who looked like he was on the firing line.

"Are you ready to tell us what happened to those blueberries?" Aunt Polly asked him softly.

Hattie felt her face flame. Dodge's chin quivered and he looked at Hattie desperately. The aunts had noticed the missing berries and they were blaming Dodge.

"I broke them," Hattie blurted out. Ruth and Polly turned again to face their niece.

"I took them into town to try to sell them at the co-op. I wanted to make some money —"

"You what?" Ruth bellowed. "You thought you could just sell the family food?"

"I picked them," Hattie tried to explain.

"You may have picked those berries, but we all work hard around here. Everyone contributes. Everybody eats. Polly doesn't cook just for herself. I don't bring in the harvest and run off to sell it for pocket money." Ruth paused for a minute. She looked about as mad as

Hattie had ever seen her. "I thought you were smarter than that, Harriet," she finished quietly.

"But I didn't sell them," Hattie said. "I was going to, but I didn't. And I wasn't trying to make pocket money." Why didn't anyone understand?

"Hattie didn't break the jars, I did," Dodge said, getting up from the table. "I didn't mean to. It was an accident."

"So you didn't sell the berries, you wasted them," Aunt Ruth said, looking straight at Hattie. "And you dragged your brother into your foolishness."

Hattie was grateful Dodge was trying to share the blame, but she wasn't sure he was making things any better. Tears stung her eyes. If wanting her family together was foolish, then maybe she was.

"I was just trying to keep Papa home," Hattie sobbed. She broke through her aunts and headed for the stairs.

She wasn't sure how long she'd been crying when she heard a knock on her door. She expected it to be Polly, but it was Ruth.

Aunt Ruth's face was serious as she came over and sat down on the bed. "I know it's hard having your papa gone," she said. "And I'm not easy to live with. I get mad and I yell and sometimes I forget to listen. But it's only because I'm trying to look out for us, Hattie. I'm doing my best. And down deep I know you are, too." She put her arm around her niece and squeezed her shoulder.

Hattie sniffed and wiped her nose on her sleeve. She knew she should say something, but she just couldn't. So they just sat there quietly for a while.

"Do you want to come down for dinner?" Ruth finally asked.

Hattie shook her head.

"I'll have Polly fix you a plate for later," Ruth said.

Hattie nodded as Ruth left the room and closed the door. Alone, Hattie rolled over and stared at the ceiling. Soon she could hear voices around the dinner table.

Hattie must have dozed off for a little bit, because she woke up to the sound of Dodge practicing his nickel horn. A tray of food was on the nightstand next to her bed. Hattie ate several spoonfuls of lukewarm soup and some bread and butter.

Feeling a little bit better, Hattie decided to work on her Christmas presents. Stashed in her closet, she had two soft squares of fabric and a needle and thread borrowed from Aunt Polly's sewing basket.

She unfolded a white cotton square and smoothed it over her knee. It was Polly's handkerchief. Hattie had taken it from Polly's drawer after Stella left. She'd been trimming it with a scrap of lace given to her by her mama, who'd used the rest on a shawl. There was just enough lace to reach around the handkerchief. She was adding an embroidered monogram, too.

With a pencil, Hattie carefully drew her aunt's initials in the corner in her best cursive. Her hand was steady.

Not even Dodge's sour notes threw her off. For the first time she felt like the Palmer handwriting method was worth the bother. Hattie was glad she'd been working extra hard on her penmanship. The letters came out smooth and curvy, just the way she'd hoped. Miss Lind would have been proud.

Using pink embroidery floss for the "P," Hattie carefully traced her lines with the chain stitch Aunt Polly had taught her last winter. She was getting better at keeping each stitch the same size, but it was slow going. And sometimes she had to take a few stitches out and start over. After a while the house grew still and Hattie felt herself getting sleepy.

Suddenly, Dodge burst into the room.

"Hattie!" he said in a loud whisper. "Hattie, what are we going to do for Frank and Abe for Christmas?"

Dodge looked as if the thought had woken him from a deep sleep. His hair stood up on one side and Hattie could see where the pillow had left creases in his cheek.

"I've got stuff for the aunts — those pinecones and frames we made in school. But what about Frank and Abe?" he went on.

Hattie tucked the handkerchief under her bedclothes — she didn't want Dodge asking any questions. Then she gave the problem her full attention.

The truth was, Hattie hadn't thought about what to do for the men, either. And they *were* like family. But they wouldn't like a spruced-up pinecone ornament or a frame decorated with dried beans. What could she and Dodge do for them that they'd really appreciate?

"I've got it," Hattie said finally. "On Christmas Eve you can sneak over and steal their boots."

Dodge squinched up his face and looked at Hattie as if she had gone mad. "That's not a very nice thing to do for Christmas."

"That's not all," Hattie explained. "You bring the boots back here and we'll shine them up, good as new. Then we can sneak them back to the bunkhouse before they wake up."

A look of understanding fell over Dodge's face, and then he laughed. "All right," he agreed excitedly. "Okay, that'll be good."

"Now go on to bed." Hattie shooed Dodge out of her room. "Tomorrow's the Christmas program."

"I know." Dodge smiled through a yawn. "I've got my solo all ready."

Hattie sighed and tucked her Christmas presents back up in the closet. She would be up late tomorrow — and maybe the next night — finishing her gifts. She was too tired to work on them anymore tonight.

Dodge played his nickel horn all the way to school the next morning, which drove Hattie a little crazy. But she had to give him credit for practicing so much. And today Hattie actually felt a little grateful that she'd been chosen to be the Archangel and not given a recitation.

She was having enough trouble completing her Christmas plans without having to memorize a whole poem, too.

As they climbed the school steps, Dodge tooted on his horn some more.

"I sought I'd play as we wok in," he explained out of the corner of his mouth.

Hattie gave her brother a look. After hearing him every night at home and all the way to school, Hattie wasn't sure she even wanted to hear his solo tonight.

With a sigh, Dodge took the hint and tucked the horn in his coat.

Inside, the schoolroom had been transformed. Miss Lind must have spent Sunday getting ready. Evergreen boughs were draped over each doorway. Stencils of gingerbread men ran around the edges of the chalkboard and in the center was a big banner wishing everyone a "Merry Christmas." A tree almost as big as the one Hattie found stood in a corner and there was even a makeshift stage set up for the program, complete with bedsheet curtains.

Hattie took her seat. She didn't feel like doing schoolwork.

But Miss Lind looked like business. "I know the Christmas program is today, but we have lots to do," she began.

The room got quiet, but Hattie could tell nobody else wanted to mind their studies today, either.

"Especially if we're going to get this tree decorated in time for a rehearsal!" Miss Lind finished with a clap of her hands.

Suddenly everyone was out of their seats and working on a project. Kids were folding, painting, stringing, and cutting decorations for the tree. Miss Lind was helping a group of older girls write out the programs.

Hattie and Jenny painted over newspaper strips with red and green paint to make paper chains. For a moment Lily stood by them. Hattie wondered if she wanted to join in. Or was she thinking that their paper chains weren't as fancy as the ones they bought in Duluth?

Hattie was in such a good mood that she considered offering Lily some paper and a brush. But when she turned around Lily was over with the girls who were working on the programs.

The day flew past. By lunch the tree was finished, programs had been made, and rehearsal had begun. By four o'clock the room was cleaned and the desks were cleared to the side to make room for everyone's families.

Most of the class gathered at the windows to see whose parents would arrive first. Fat snowflakes began to drift down. Then sleigh bells began to ring. It was Mr. and Mrs. Soma, with bells tied to their horses. Soon the rest of the parents were hurrying inside to warm up and put their potluck dishes by the fire.

Hattie helped her aunts with their coats. They settled into two seats just before the program started.

Dodge and the Teeny Weeny Band opened the show. Although Hattie had heard him play his "Little Drummer Boy" solo a million times, she was pretty sure this was the first time he hit all the right notes in the right order.

Hattie peeked out past the curtain to see what the audience thought. Sure enough, even Aunt Ruth, who just a few nights before had threatened to bury the horn and put it out of its misery, enjoyed Dodge's playing. When the song was over, everyone clapped loudly.

After making it through her entrance and exit in the Nativity without tripping on her costume, Hattie snuck out to sit between her aunts and watch the rest of the program. As relieved as she was that her part was over, she still felt a pang of envy when Lily took the stage.

At first Lily looked a little nervous, but after "and all through the house" every trace of nerves was gone. She did the whole poem without stumbling or missing a word. And the most impressive part was that she never looked at her feet or off to the side. She looked at everyone in the audience, just like a real actress. Miss Lind didn't once have to put her hands up to her ears at the back of the room, the signal for the students to talk louder.

Too soon the program was over. Now it was time to eat!

Hattie ducked behind the stove to get Aunt Polly's dish. She was hungry and everything smelled delicious. Lily and Mrs. Swenson set their pan of potatoes and cream next to Polly's rutabeggy-and-bacon casserole.

"You must have used at least a dozen potatoes!" Hattie heard Lily whisper to her mom.

She had not meant to eavesdrop, but suddenly Hattie remembered what she'd heard the day before at the Jungle. In all of the excitement she had almost forgotten about the Swensons' low food supply. A dozen potatoes was a real sacrifice.

Hattie felt terrible. Here she'd been assuming the worst about Lily, when the girl was probably having a hard enough time adjusting to country life. And Hattie had gone and yelled at her!

Soon the table was full of all kinds of casseroles, stews, and even a turkey! Everyone hovered around the buffet and filled plates with the homemade food.

"Hattie, over here!" Jenny Soma waved Hattie toward a corner where she and some other kids were eating. Hattie started toward them with her plate, then paused. Should she invite Lily to join them?

Hattie turned to see if Lily was still behind her, but saw that she'd already found a seat next to her parents and baby sister. The whole family was bent over their food. The way they were eating it didn't look like they'd be interested in talking.

The mood in the schoolhouse was festive as families

enjoyed the delicious potluck. Before long, the conversation turned to the weather.

Outside, the slow puffy snowflakes had hardened into more serious snow. The wind howled and windows rattled. Adults peered into the storm and talked about heading out while they could still see enough to get home.

"I don't think this snow is kidding around," Mr. Soma remarked.

After sharing Christmas wishes, everyone started to pack up their dishes and leftover food and load their wagons.

The wind was howling and the snow was blowing when Hattie and her family got outside. She was sad that the party was over but anxious to get home, too. She hadn't been in the mood to join in the talk with the other kids about what they might get for Christmas. She was still feeling bad about Lily and her family.

Waiting in the wagon was cold. Hattie buried her face in her scarf to keep off the pelting snow. What was taking Aunt Ruth so long? Hattie looked up and saw that Ruth was talking to someone's dad in front of the wagon next to theirs. Hattie wasn't sure who it was. She squinted at the child in the wagon's seat and realized it was Lily. She was holding her baby sister.

Lily was looking right at her. Hattie had to say something.

"You, uh, did a good job on your poem," Hattie said through her muffler.

85

"What?" Lily yelled back. The wind and the noise of the families getting ready to go was too much.

"Merry Christmas!" Hattie said, louder.

Lily's face lit up. "Merry Christmas to you, too!" she yelled back.

"I think we've dallied long enough," Aunt Ruth proclaimed, cutting off the conversation and climbing up next to Hattie. "Let's get this show on the road."

"I'm going to take Oliver Swenson out hunting as soon as this storm clears up," Ruth said to Polly when they'd pulled away from the school. "Poor man says he's having no luck."

They were almost halfway home when Ruth spoke again. "Frankly, I'm worried about the Swensons."

Nobody said anything, but Hattie knew exactly how Aunt Ruth felt.

Chapter Thirteen
The Big Storm

The wind was still howling and snow was still coming down the next morning. Hattie tried to see how much snow they'd gotten overnight but couldn't see a thing out of her snow-plastered windows.

It was Christmas Eve. Downstairs, Dodge was whooping and hollering with excitement. Upstairs, Hattie didn't feel the least bit like whooping. She was tired and worried. She'd stayed up late working on Christmas presents and had managed to finish hemming a bandanna for Ruth. But even though she'd wished as hard as she could, she hadn't managed to make the snow stop. In fact, the storm hadn't even slowed.

There was no way Papa could make it home now. And no way the Swensons would have fresh game on their Christmas table.

The smell of warm biscuits drifted up from the kitchen. Hattie pulled on her thick stockings, sweater, and jumper and tramped downstairs. She was just sitting down when Ruth, Frank, and Abe came into the kitchen. They'd been out shoveling so they could get to the barn and the bunkhouse.

Dodge was so excited he could barely stay in his seat.

"What are you squirming around for?" Abe asked. "You excited or something?"

"You don't think Santa can find your place in this muck, do you?" Frank gestured toward the outside with his usual smile and wink.

Aunt Polly noticed how glum Hattie looked and gave her shoulder a squeeze. "He'll find it just fine," she said.

"He couldn't ever forget you two scalawags," Ruth chimed in. "Maybe he'll just be a little late is all."

Hattie silently wondered if her aunts were really talking about Papa.

The breakfast table was loaded with biscuits and butter and eggs. Hattie dug in with the others. But after a few bites all she could think of was Lily and her family wolfing down their dinners the night before. Hard times were on everybody, but Hattie had never known what it was like to be hungry. She took another bite of her biscuit, but couldn't swallow. She needed to tell her family what she'd heard about the Swensons.

Washing her biscuit down with a gulp of milk, she stood up.

"We've got to help the Swensons," she blurted. "I think they may be starving."

Everyone at the table stopped chewing and talking and stared at Hattie.

"I know I said I was worried, but the Swensons aren't starving," Ruth said calmly. "Mr. Swenson told me they had plenty of food put by. They'll be okay."

"No. I heard all about it when I was down at the Jungle. They don't have anything in their smokehouse. And last night Lily acted like she hadn't seen food like that in months. I think Mrs. Swenson used the last of their potatoes to make their dish to bring to school and I know they won't have anything for Christmas dinner . . ." Hattie trailed off. She didn't know why she was so worried about the new family — why it meant so much — but it did.

"We have to help them," she said as her eyes began to sting.

"What in the world were you doing at the Jungle?" Ruth asked, her eyebrows heading south.

Polly shushed her sister. "I think helping the Swensons is a fine idea, don't you, Ruth? It's the season of giving."

Ruth unfurled her eyebrows and mashed her lips together, biting back what she wanted to say before agreeing with her sister. "Indeed, I do. I was thinking about taking them a rabbit or two. We've got more than enough meat in the smokehouse. I'll go directly after breakfast."

Hattie started to feel a little better. "I can take them some blueberries," she volunteered.

"Now wait a minute. We don't both need to go out in this storm. I'll take them the berries, too. You can stay here with your brother." Ruth cleared her plate from the table.

"I want to take them myself," Hattie insisted.

Polly looked like she was about to intervene again when Ruth conceded.

"Are your chores done? You'll have to dress warm, you know. It's a long walk."

"I know." Hattie felt relieved. The Swensons would have something to eat, and she wouldn't have to spend the day sitting around wishing for Papa.

By the time Hattie was dressed, Ruth had the rabbits in a sack and Polly had packed up some pantry staples.

"Can I go, too?" Dodge asked as they pulled on their boots.

"I think Hattie and I can handle this one without you," Ruth teased. "You keep an eye on Aunt Polly's fire. She has a lot of cooking to do today."

The walk was long and cold, but there was a lull in the storm so the snow slowed. The wind, though, kept gusting up, blowing fallen snow around and making it too hard to talk. Luckily, it stayed mostly at their backs and didn't make the trail much slower going.

Hattie was happy to keep quiet. As she trudged in Ruth's big boot-steps she wondered where Papa was and if he was warm and fed. Maybe he was warming his hands around a fire with some hobos, like the men she'd met in the Jungle. Maybe he was sitting on a train stopped somewhere between here and Utah. Thinking of Papa stranded and hungry made her feel even more determined to get the food she was carrying to the Swensons. At least she could make sure *someone* got fed.

Hattie could tell by the look on his face that Mr. Swenson was surprised to see her and Aunt Ruth standing at his front door.

"Come in, come in," he stammered. "I would have thought it was too snowy to hunt."

Ruth and Hattie laid down their bags and peeled off their hats and coats.

"We're not here for hunting, Oliver. This is just a Christmas visit," Ruth explained.

Lily was sitting with her mom and baby sister next to a low-burning fire. Hattie took the blueberries from her sack over to her.

Hattie wanted to say something to make up for not being very nice to the new girl since she'd moved to town. But all she could manage was, "These are for you."

"Thank you." Surprise showed on Lily's face as she took the jar. "I know these berries are worth a lot —"

"But we don't accept charity." Mr. Swenson cut her off, taking the jar and handing it back to Hattie.

"It's not charity, Mr. Swenson. It's . . ." Hattie wasn't sure what it was. Somehow this was different from taking something for nothing. There was no shame in it.

"It's just how we do things out here," Ruth explained. "Neighbors help neighbors."

Mr. Swenson put the jar down on the table. He didn't look convinced. But before he could say anything, Mrs. Swenson got up and handed the baby to her husband.

"Well, we thank you for it," she stated plainly. "And we're grateful to have such nice neighbors. Now, can I offer you something hot to drink after that long cold walk?"

Hattie had been hoping for something warm. She was still freezing from being outside and the Swensons' house was chilly, too.

Lily got up to get some wood for the fire and Ruth motioned that Hattie should help. Outside the back door a dozen logs were stacked on a small porch.

"Is that all of your wood?" Hattie asked, surprised.

Lily jumped. She didn't know Hattie had come with her. "Uh-huh," she mumbled. "We had coal heat in Duluth." Hattie could tell Lily was looking at her, waiting to see how she would react. The last time she'd mentioned Duluth, Hattie had yelled at her.

"We've never had coal heat," Hattie said. Her face flushed as she remembered that day in Iron Creek.

"We weren't sure how long wood would last. We're trying to save what we have for cooking until this storm passes. But don't worry. We can spare some for a hot drink."

Hattie nodded, but she wasn't so sure. It didn't look to her like they had enough wood to last through the night and into tomorrow. What if the storm lasted for several days?

As the girls carried in a few logs and some kindling, a great idea suddenly sprang into Hattie's head. She hoped Aunt Ruth would like it, too.

Hattie didn't know what Ruth had said while she and Lily were getting the wood, but when they came back in Mrs. Swenson was putting Polly's staples into their cupboards, exclaiming over the generosity of each gift. "We haven't had molasses since we left Duluth," she said, smiling.

Mr. Swenson still looked a little grumpy. In a funny way he reminded Hattie of Aunt Ruth. Aunt Polly would have called it pride.

"I just wish there was a way we could pay you back for this favor," he said.

Hattie couldn't hold back any longer. "You can!" she practically shouted. "You can come spend Christmas with us!"

Chapter Fourteen
Good Neighbors

Everyone was surprised by Hattie's invitation. The room was momentarily silent except for the baby's coos. Lily looked hopefully from Hattie to her parents. Aunt Ruth looked like a trout the way she was opening and closing her mouth. But she recovered quickly.

"That's right," Ruth said. "My little sister isn't able to join us and we have plenty of space —"

"And food," Hattie chimed in.

"We'd be delighted if you'd join us overnight," Ruth finished.

Oliver Swenson could not deny the hopeful looks on the faces of his wife and daughter.

"It'll give the kids a chance to get to know each other," Ruth continued. "And maybe I can give you some tips — I do pride myself on knowing a few things about north country hunting and farming."

Hattie was amazed at Ruth's soft touch. She could be as charming as Aunt Polly when she wanted to be.

The hard look in Mr. Swenson's eyes disappeared. "We'd be pleased to join you," he said quietly. "But only if you'll let us help. Lotta here is an amazing cook. And I, well, I may be an old cabinetmaker and a fledgling farmer, but I can do just about anything that needs doing."

"Don't you worry, Oliver." Ruth smiled a little sideways at her new friend. "That's rule number one: Everybody works on a farm."

There was a lot to do before they could leave the Swensons'. Hattie helped Lily and Mrs. Swenson bundle up baby Helen. Then Hattie banked the fire while they packed up a few clothes and Ruth helped Mr. Swenson get the horses ready.

The Swensons only had two old plow horses and it was too snowy to ride them. They didn't want to leave them in the barn while they were gone, so they loaded their small amount of gear on the animals' backs and led them through the drifts.

The walk back seemed to take twice as long as the walk there. The wind was in their faces this time and the horses — who weren't anxious to be out in such a storm — pulled back in protest. Aunt Ruth and Mr. Swenson broke the trail, tugging on the horses' leads to urge them on. Mrs. Swenson followed with baby Helen tucked snug against her chest, inside her jacket. Hattie and Lily brought up the rear.

Hattie still hadn't managed to apologize to Lily for yelling at her in town. She hoped Lily wasn't mad and being nice because the adults were around. But out here it was too cold and windy for talking.

When they got to the house, Polly, Dodge, Frank, and Abe were all waiting for them.

"Here we thought you were lost and really you were just getting recruits," Frank teased as Ruth introduced everyone to the Swensons. "It's a good thing, too. You had Polly here so worried she's been cooking for an army!"

Frank laughed and winked at Aunt Polly. Aunt Polly just smiled back.

Ruth and Abe took Mr. Swenson out to the barn to settle the horses, and Polly led Mrs. Swenson and baby Helen to the fire to get warm. Baby Helen sat on a blanket near the hearth, entertained by Frank and Dodge, who made silly faces at her.

Hattie was glad everyone was enjoying the company and hoped her idea wouldn't create too much extra work for her aunts. As soon as she could feel her fingers again she started upstairs to make up additional beds. Dodge was going to bunk with Hattie and Lily so Lily's parents and baby Helen could have Dodge's room.

"Need some help?" Lily asked, trailing behind.

Hattie nodded. This was her chance to say something.

"Is this your aunts' farm?" Lily asked before Hattie could speak.

Hattie nodded again.

"It sure is nice. You live here with them long?"

96

"Two years —" Hattie was about to say more but Lily interrupted.

"I'm not really used to farm life yet. Mama says it'll get easier. But it sure feels hard sometimes," Lily said. "Mama's family used to farm, but I was born in Duluth. I lived there my whole life — until I moved here."

Hattie got out extra sheets and blankets. Lily Swenson sure was a talker! If Hattie was going to get a word in she had to do it fast.

Pushing a pile of blankets into Lily arms, Hattie finally broke in.

"Look, I know it hasn't been easy for you to be new here and all. I know I haven't made it any better. And I'm really sorry about yelling at you in town the other day, but I wasn't trying to make extra pocket money. I was trying to make my papa able to stay home. He's always traveling. He's been trying to make money for the farm ever since Mama died and it seems like he's been gone forever."

Hattie hadn't meant to tell Lily everything. She had only thought to apologize. But before she realized it *she* was the one talking up a storm.

Luckily, Lily was as good a listener as she was a talker. By the time they finished making up the beds and arranging a dresser drawer for Helen in Dodge's room it was time for dinner. Hattie already felt like she and Lily had been friends for a long time.

Aunt Polly's stew tasted especially good around a full table, and after dinner Frank brought out his accordion. Dodge started upstairs for his horn but Aunt Ruth pulled him back and onto her lap.

"Oh no you don't," she teased. "Tonight we're listening to a different musician!"

Frank played some songs Hattie didn't know and then some carols she did. When Frank played "Silent Night," Mr. Swenson sang along. His voice was deep and rich. Outside the storm was quiet. When the song was finished the only sound was the crackle of the fire.

Lily got up from the floor where she'd been playing pick-up-sticks with Hattie and crawled onto her daddy's lap.

In all the excitement Hattie had almost forgotten about her own papa. She had almost stopped missing him. Now, seeing her new friend in her father's lap in her own living room was almost too much to bear. Tomorrow it would be Christmas. Christmas without Papa.

While Frank started "Oh, Little Town of Bethlehem," Hattie said her good-nights and headed upstairs to bed. She would have liked some company, but Dodge was dozing on Aunt Ruth's lap and Lily looked comfortable on her father's knee. Hattie didn't feel like listening to any more Christmas music. Besides, she still had to finish her aunts' gifts.

Alone in her room, Hattie put the last bit of stitching on Aunt Ruth's bandanna and wrapped it up, securing it with red yarn. She only had the "E" — one last letter — to embroider on Aunt Polly's handkerchief.

A stray gust of wind blew the frozen tree branches outside Hattie's window, and they brushed against the glass. Hattie jumped and thought of the freezing weather outside and her long, cold walk earlier in the day. It would be even colder at night. She wondered about the men in the Jungle. What would happen to them on a night like this? And what about her papa? If he was caught out in the storm trying to get home, he could get frostbite — or worse.

Hattie's eyes blurred. She couldn't see the stitching. She felt awful for wishing her papa would come home in this storm. What if he was freezing somewhere just because he was trying to get to her and Dodge? Maybe he was really better off in Salt Lake City without them.

A sob escaped Hattie's chest. Her needle jerked. Horrified, Hattie realized she'd torn the delicate cotton handkerchief. It was too much. Choking back more sobs, Hattie threw the hankie down and buried her face in her pillow so nobody would hear her cry.

Chapter Fifteen
The Best Surprise

When Hattie opened her eyes the next morning, she was snuggled in her cozy bed under a pile of quilts and blankets. Lily was already up, and Dodge's bedclothes lay in a rumpled heap next to his unmade bed.

Wrapped in an afghan, Lily was looking out the window at the giant drifts of snow. "It's finally stopped," she said. "And it's beautiful. The whitest Christmas ever."

Hattie sat up with a start. It was Christmas, and her gifts weren't finished yet! She must have fallen asleep. Suddenly she remembered ripping her aunt's handkerchief the night before.

Hattie leaped out of bed and pulled up the covers. Then she began to search the floor for the ripped handkerchief. Maybe she could salvage it before breakfast.

Hattie got down on her hands and knees to look under the bed, but the hankie wasn't there. She was about to really panic when she spotted something white on her bedside table. It was the handkerchief — the rip neatly stitched up and the last bit of embroidery finished.

Hattie stared at the handkerchief for a minute, then looked up at Lily.

"Elves," Lily said with a smile.

It was still early, so the girls took their time getting dressed and then braided each other's hair. Hattie wove Lily's thick blond hair into two braids and neatly twisted them into a bun. Then Lily wove Hattie's dark hair into a fancy French braid down the middle of her back.

Soon, familiar voices and the smell of Ruth's homemade sausage cooking drifted up to the second floor of the farmhouse. The two girls hurried out of Hattie's room and headed down the hall. As they approached the stairs, Hattie could hear Dodge shouting on the other side of the door. Who could blame him? It was Christmas, after all.

At the bottom of the stairs, Lily slipped her hand into Hattie's. Hattie sighed. Even without Papa, this was going to be a special Christmas.

Squeezing Lily's hand, Hattie pushed open the kitchen door. "What's all the ruckus?" she shouted to her brother. "You'd think it was Chris —"

Hattie stopped short. For there, sitting at the kitchen table, was Papa.

Hattie's heart leaped in her chest. And then she flew across the kitchen, into Papa's strong, open arms.

"Papa," Hattie said, barely believing that this was for real. Was he really here? How could he have made it through the storm? She had so much she wanted to tell him — so many things to share. But nothing came out. All she could do was bury her head against his chest and say "Papa."

"Quit hogging him," Dodge complained after a few minutes. "I want a hug, too."

"You've already had at least ten," Aunt Ruth reminded him. She was standing by the fire with the Swensons, smiling and sipping her coffee.

Hattie laughed and wiped the tears from her eyes. "Oh, all right, Dodge," she agreed.

"I can hug both of you munchkins at once!" Papa declared with a grin. "'Cept I might accidentally squeeze you so hard that you break!"

Dodge piled onto Papa's lap with Hattie and they both got the squeeze of their lives.

"Careful, Ned," Polly said with a laugh. "You wouldn't want to do anything that would keep those kids from their stockings."

"Stockings?" Papa echoed. "Are you telling me that Santa thought these two rascals were *good* this year?"

"We were, Papa!" Dodge shouted earnestly. "Honest!"

"Hmmm," Papa replied. "I'll have to think. Is that what I've heard, or not?" He winked at Hattie.

"Well, if you want my opinion —" Aunt Ruth began.

"I didn't mean to break the berries or spill the sugar," Dodge shouted. "Those were accidents!"

"— these two kids were good as gold," Ruth finished. "Mostly."

"And I think I saw more than coal in those stockings hanging by the fireplace," Aunt Polly added.

Dodge and Hattie raced into the living room to the mantel. There were stockings for everyone, even Lily and baby Helen.

"This is for you," Hattie said, handing Lily the stocking.

Lily's blue eyes lit up. "Really?" she asked. She took the stocking gratefully. "Thanks."

The bigger kids — including Dodge this year — got tablets of paper and two pencils each. They also each got a small paper sack full of peanuts, and a few curly hard candies. Baby Helen got a small rag doll and an apple. She cooed at the doll and stuffed its foot into her drooly mouth.

Hattie divided up the hard candies she had left from Carlbom's Candy Kitchen between Lily and Dodge.

"Thank you!" Lily whispered as she eyed the licorice bites. She told Hattie they were her favorite, and she hadn't had a single one since she'd moved to Iron Creek.

Then Hattie handed her aunts each a small package wrapped in newsprint and tied with yarn.

Ruth tore the paper off a bright red bandanna. "How'd you know I've been needing a new bandanna?" she asked, giving Hattie a squeeze.

Hattie shrugged. She couldn't help but grin as Ruth took a closer look and spied her initials and the cross-stitch "X"s and "O"s that ran along the edges of the cloth.

"I have a feeling you'll have to use that right away, Ruth," Polly said gently. Sure enough, a second later Ruth was wiping her eyes and hurrying to stoke the already big fire.

Polly opened her gift carefully, saving the paper and unknotting the yarn.

"My handkerchief!" she cried delightedly as she finally pulled it out. "It's bloomed!"

Hattie giggled as she got another good hug.

"It's beautiful, Hattie. Thank you," her aunt whispered in her ear. "And your stitches are perfect."

Suddenly the door was thrown open, and Frank and Abe rushed into the living room.

"Santa stole our boots!" Abe declared.

Everyone looked down at their feet. The men were wearing nothing but very snowy socks!

With a gasp, Dodge leaped up and scurried out the door. A moment later he returned with the men's boots — blackened and brightly polished.

"It was an accident," Dodge exclaimed. "Honest!"

Hattie grinned at Dodge. He must have carried out their plan — or at least part of it — while she was asleep. In her worry she'd forgotten all about it. She noticed Lily, who was eating her nuts by the fireplace and grinning. Maybe the elves had helped Dodge out, too.

"We're just glad that Santa hasn't turned to a life of crime," Frank said, sounding relieved.

Everyone had a good laugh. Then Frank and Abe hung their snow-covered stockings by the fire, and the families sat down to eggs, sausage, butter, and scones.

Chapter Sixteen
Home for the Holidays

Farm chores didn't take a holiday — not even on Christmas. So after breakfast there was work for everyone to do.

Lily and her mom helped Aunt Polly with the dishes. Mr. Swenson and Frank chopped some wood, while Dodge carried a day's supply into the house. Ruth and Abe had to see to something out in the shed.

Hattie was desperate to have her papa to herself for a few minutes so she could give him her surprise, but she noticed that he looked tired. He must've traveled day and night for several days running to get home — especially with the storm.

"Why don't you rest in the living room while I do my chores?" Hattie suggested.

But Papa was already going for his coat. "I didn't come home to sit around on my duff," he said. "And besides, I think you're just the girl to help me brush up on barn chores."

Hattie grinned and pulled on her coat and hat. "I can do that," she said. "I have to run upstairs and get something first. I'll be right back."

Hattie dashed up the stairs and down the hall to her room. Pulling out her mason jar full of money, she poured it into a sock and tied it up. Then she stuffed it into her coat pocket.

Thoroughly bundled, Hattie and her papa headed past the snowdrifts to the barn. It was obvious from the huge piles of snow that Frank, Abe, and Ruth had worked hard to clear the paths.

Inside the barn, it was a little warmer. Hattie showed her papa how to break the ice on the water with a sharp stick, where the feed was for the horses, pigs, and cows, and how much each animal got to eat.

"The cows have finally gone dry. So there's no milking to do," Hattie explained. "I miss the fresh milk, but not so much the milking."

Papa grinned. "You sure know your way around this barn," he said, impressed. "Seems like it was just last spring that you needed help with all of this."

"Running a farm is lots of work," Hattie replied. "Everyone has to pitch in."

"You sound like your Aunt Ruth," Papa teased, tugging on the end of her scarf.

Hattie supposed he was right. But just then, she didn't mind being like Aunt Ruth so much. Aunt Ruth was strong, and could take care of things — lots of things. Hattie wanted to be like that, too.

Hattie couldn't contain herself any longer. She pulled out the sock full of money and handed it to her papa.

"This is for you," she told him in a rush. "So you can stay home for a while. It's just over four dollars. I wanted to get more, but I couldn't. Merry Christmas, Papa."

Hattie beamed at her papa, but then realized he didn't look happy. He was staring at the sock, his mouth turned down at the corners. He stared at that sock for a long time. Finally he wrapped his arms around Hattie and gave her a giant hug.

"Thank you," he whispered. Then he held Hattie at arm's length and looked her square in the face. "But a man has to take care of his family. I'm not a farmer, Hattie. And I know you and your aunts don't need much help. But I have to do what I can, in my own way — even if it means being away from here, and you kids, right now."

Hattie tried not to cry as her father hugged her again — even more tightly than before.

"I'm so proud of you, Hattie," he said. "And I know your mama would be, too. But I want you to keep this money for yourself. You'll find a good use for it. I know you will."

Hattie let out a loud sniffle. She managed a nod.

"Now chin up, Miss," Papa said, pretending to be stern. He looked at Hattie for another long moment, as if he were thinking about something. Then he grinned. "We have to get these chores done so we can get back inside and plan our week together!"

"A week?" Hattie exclaimed. Usually Papa was only

home for two or three days before heading off again. A week was seven whole days! And school would be out for half of it, so they'd have even more time together!

"On to stall mucking!" Hattie pronounced gleefully. She handed Papa a manure rake and sent him into Chestnut's stall before moving on to another one herself. Soon they were finished, and ready to head back into the house to warm up and tell everyone the news about Papa's stay.

Only as soon as she stepped out of the barn, Hattie was pelted by a giant snowball!

"Sorry, Hat," Dodge shouted. "I was going for Aunt Ruth!"

Hattie looked in the other direction and spotted Aunt Ruth and Lily behind a snowbank, firing away at Dodge, Abe, and Frank.

"Hattie, we need you!" Ruth bellowed.

Hattie scrambled over the snowbank just as Papa got whammoed by Lily, who was an ace with a snowball.

That was the end of the regular rematch. The fight became a free-for-all, with everyone throwing snowballs at everyone else. Before long the Swensons and Aunt Polly came out of the house to see what the ruckus was about — and got into the action as well.

Soon the whole crew had snow in their faces, up their sleeves, and down their backs. Red-cheeked and laughing, they stumbled into the house to warm up by the fire.

"I'm freezing," Dodge chattered as he stripped off his mittens.

"Serves you right," Hattie teased, "thinking you could take on Aunt Ruth."

"It wasn't my idea!" Dodge protested. "It was Frank's!"

"Now, don't you go getting me into this," Frank said, putting on an innocent face. "I was just out there chopping wood." He tousled Dodge's hair, and everyone chuckled. They all knew that Frank and Dodge were *both* troublemakers when it came to snowball fights.

"It's going to be a while before dinner," Aunt Polly piped up. "How about some hot chocolate to warm up?"

The kids all accepted the offer gratefully. And while they were sipping — or guzzling, in Dodge's case — Aunt Ruth barreled through the door with a Christmas surprise almost as good as Papa's: a sleek new sled with waxed runners and space for two!

"A sled! A sled!" Dodge cheered.

Hattie ran her finger over one of the runners. It was as smooth as a cow's udder. "It's beautiful," she breathed.

Aunt Polly nodded knowingly. "So *that's* what you've been up to out in that shed of yours," she said.

Aunt Ruth nodded. "I had a little help," she admitted. "Frank here is a talented woodworker."

"I was only the assistant!" Frank insisted.

Aunt Polly beamed at Frank, and Hattie and Dodge hugged Aunt Ruth and Frank in thanks.

"Looks like we'll be doing lots of sledding this week," Papa proclaimed.

"Papa is going to stay a whole week!" Hattie burst out.

Everyone cheered — Dodge and Hattie most of all.

Then Lily whispered something in Hattie's ear. Dinner was almost ready, but there was just enough time for the kids to reprise their parts from the Christmas pageant for Frank, Abe, and Papa.

The mini-show was a hit. Dodge only played two wrong notes, and Hattie got to recite the part of "The Night Before Christmas" she had memorized before Lily finished it off. They didn't make a single mistake!

When the performance was over, Hattie wasn't sure who clapped the loudest, Papa or Frank.

Finally it was time for dinner. Hungry, everyone squeezed around the kitchen table to eat.

Papa carved the ham while Mrs. Swenson ladled her special mustard sauce into Aunt Polly's fancy silver bowl. There was a platter heaped with roasted carrots and winter squash, a bowl full of mashed potatoes, and two loaves of warm homemade bread.

Hattie was squished between Dodge and Lily at one end of the table. A week ago, she would have thought that was a terrible place to be. But as she looked at the happy faces surrounding her — including Papa's — she was happy. This was truly the best Christmas ever.

About the Authors

Jane B. Mason grew up in Duluth, Minnesota, but now lives in Oakland, California. Sarah Hines Stephens grew up in Twain Harte, California, but now lives in Oakland as well. In fact, it's just an eleven-minute drive from one house to the other. Jane and Sarah are good friends who enjoy writing books for kids both together and separately. Some of their books include *The Little Mermaid and Other Stories*, *Heidi*, *Paul Bunyan and Other Tall Tales*, *The Legend of Sleepy Hollow*, *The Nutcracker*, *The Jungle Book*, and *King Arthur*, all Scholastic Junior Classics, and The Princess School series. Between them they have two husbands, three kids, three dogs, and one cat.

HAVE AN ABBY DAY!

Meet Abby Hayes, your typical amazing fifth grader and the star of a series that's as fresh and funny as Abby herself!

Make your own calendar on Abby's Web site....
www.scholastic.com/titles/abbyhayes

Have you read them all?

- ❏ **Abby Hayes #1:** Every Cloud Has a Silver Lining
- ❏ **Abby Hayes #2:** The Declaration of Independence
- ❏ **Abby Hayes #3:** Reach for the Stars
- ❏ **Abby Hayes #4:** Have Wheels, Will Travel
- ❏ **Abby Hayes #5:** Look Before You Leap
- ❏ **Abby Hayes #6:** The Pen Is Mightier Than the Sword
- ❏ **Abby Hayes #7:** Two Heads Are Better Than One
- ❏ **Abby Hayes #8:** The More, the Merrier
- ❏ **Abby Hayes #9:** Out of Sight, Out of Mind
- ❏ **Abby Hayes #10:** Everything New Under the Sun
- ❏ **Abby Hayes #11:** Too Close for Comfort
- ❏ **Abby Hayes #12:** Good Things Come in Small Packages

📖 SCHOLASTIC

ABB0404

When everything falls apart, the best thing to do is to stick together.

Ann M. Martin, author of
A Corner of the Universe

☐ HC: 0-439-09823-8 • $16.95 /$23.99 Can.

☐ PB: 0-439-09824-6 • $5.99/$8.99 Can.

Belle Teal's life isn't easy, but she gets by. She lives with her mother and grandmother far out in the country. They don't have much money, but she feels rich with their love. However, as a new school year begins, Belle Teal faces unexpected challenges and big problems.

Ella. Snow. Rapunzel. Rose.
Four friends who wait for no prince.